D1452343

Who Would Have Thunk It!

The *First Adventures*
of the
Fraser Foster Kids

written by George C. Fraser
and Emma Fraser-Pendleton
with *Jerry Craft*

illustrations
by Jerry Craft

FraserNet Publishing Group • Cleveland

Inquiries should be addressed to:
FraserNet Publishing Group
2940 Noble Rd. #203
Cleveland, Ohio 44121

Visit us on the web at http://frasernet.com/

Summary: The story of Emma, George and Joseph Fraser — three siblings who were placed in the foster care system after their mother became mentally ill and their father could no longer care for them. Based on fact, the story follows the trio as they bounce from one home to another looking for a family to call their own.

ISBN: 978-0-9856218-0-3

ISBN-10: 098562180X

Library of Congress Control Number: 2012939471

First Edition
Printed in the United States of America

Who Would Have Thunk It!
by George C. Fraser & Emma Fraser-Pendleton
with Jerry Craft

FraserNet Publishing Group

---

to Joseph,
Always loved
Never forgotten

Foreword
by George and Emma

Some people think that foster families are these amazing folks who just want to help needy children. And you know what? A lot of them are. But those weren't the ones that we ever got. It's not that WE were bad, it's because THEY were just bad people! Sometimes they said bad words and sometimes they even hit us. It made us wonder why people who didn't even like kids took us in. It wasn't until later that we realized that it was about money. You see, the city gave families a monthly check for every child they took in. So the more foster kids you had — the bigger their check. As luck would have it, we always wound up with those folks who did it for the money. We used to say, "when we grow up, we were going to write a book and tell the world what it's like to be foster children. Our book would be called, Children for Rent." I guess this is that book.

But first let us explain. The story you are about to read is a story from the heart of how we wished it could have been, but never really was. It's a story of hope and how three little foster kids finally find a family, a dog named Sidney, and finally find love. Although it never really happened that way for us, it CAN for lots of kids. Our story is not fact, or fiction, and that's why we invented the word factional. I guess you can say, it's a sort of a fairy tale based on our experiences.

Our story began a very long time ago when we were little kids with no place to live. Our mother got sick and our father had to give us up, so we were put into a shelter — and then foster homes. We were in foster homes for 13 years! It was very hard, but we made it.

Now that we're adults, we wanted to share our story with other kids who have been in foster homes, and even kids who have had a tough life.

The part about Mr. and Mrs. Morris, well ... we made that whole part up. In fact, most of the happy stuff is made up because our lives as foster kids was not a happy one. Besides, who wants to read a story without some good stuff?

During the time we lived in foster homes, we did meet other kids who were happy and who had nice foster parents — like three of our older brothers: Walter, Edward and Scottie. They lived in a foster home with really nice people. I mean REALLY nice people! So, we are thankful for those good folks out there who have provided really loving homes, because a loving home is the most precious thing that an adult can give to a child.

The lessons we learned from our time as foster kids have helped us to grow up and be good human beings, and that is why we can now share our story. They are simple lessons, and we have tried to live our lives based on them:

- *Never lose hope.*
- *Rejection prepares you for perfection.*
- *Never lose your faith in a higher power, because a strong faith will take you through anything!*

It worked for us.

This is our story and we are sticking to it!

Our Family History
by George

We didn't know anything about the rest of our family. Basically at that point in our lives, we had only four family members: Our Dad, and our three older brothers: Walter, Edward and Scottie, who lived in a different foster home in Queens. That's in New York. We only got to see our brothers at Christmas time and when our Dad would take us to the amusement park every summer. Those were some of the best days of our lives. When we got older, Dad introduced us to his mother — our Grandmother. She was a very scary person (or so it seemed). She lived in England, and one Christmas she came to stay with us while we were at our annual Christmas stay with Dad. *OMIGOSH!* That woman never seemed to smile, and we sort of tip-toed around her. I do remember this: she made us stay in bed real late on Christmas, and we hated that! Dad always let us get up at the crack of dawn and open our gifts; Grandma was having none of that! Said that, "little kids need their rest."

As far as the rest our family, we didn't know about them, not until years later. And do you know the strange thing about meeting them? They would sort of just drop by our dad's house in Brooklyn, and dad would say, "This is your older brother." It happened just like that! In total our mother had eleven kids, but they all lived with other people. We sure as heck didn't understand any of those dynamics at the time. In fact, to us, it was what it was, and we just accepted the fact that we were part of this big family. Nobody used last names, and it was not until years later when we were older did we discover that our mother had been married several times before she had married our dad, Walter Frederick Fraser; and that she had also had some kids when she wasn't married.

Life was different for us, always had been, so it was no big deal. Besides, living in foster homes and being moved around from family to family made us numb to stuff like that. So, here's the final deal regarding our family: Mom had six kids with our dad, and we also had four older brothers and one older sister who lived in Ohio (who we didn't meet until we were in our late teens). Never met a grandfather, guess they all died along the way. Dad had some sisters, who we met when we were much older, and we also had some cousins. They all lived in England, and from time to time, they would visit our dad, and that's how we got to meet them.

We met our mom when Emma was nine, I was eight, and Joseph was seven. Dad took us to see her in the hospital. It was a place in Brooklyn. That was a horrible day. Dad had shown us pictures of our Mom, and she was tall and real pretty. But the woman we met looked nothing like the picture we had seen. She was dressed in old clothes, and her long pretty hair was tied in knots, and she didn't even remember our names. Poor Joseph, she didn't even know who he was. Dad had to introduce him, and Mom said he was, "real black," because she drank Maxwell House Coffee when she was pregnant with him. Emma and I were very light (looked white, with straight hair), but our four other brothers were brown-skinned with kinky hair. That's when we realized that our mother was mentally ill and she would spend the rest of her life in Kings County Hospital for the mentally disturbed. Dad told us that mom was in the hospital for thirty-seven years. When she died in her seventies, it was the first and only time that all of her children were in the same place at one time. Except for our brother Howard. We heard that he had been shot to death in a poker game. No one told us, we just heard folks talking.

I remember at our mother's funeral, that Emma, Joseph and I cried, not because we knew her, but because we never really knew her — that is, knew her when she was sane, and pretty like the picture we had seen as children. Both of our parents died from heart attacks. Dad died two years before Mom, also in his seventies; but his death was not as hard on us as our Mom's. I think it was because we knew him, and he was always in our lives. I know that sounds backwards, but that's how it was. Today, all of Mom's children that are still living keep in touch. Sort of. Bet that would surprise her.

My little brother, Joseph, was killed in his early forties, the police told us it was a drug-related killing. Because of complications too painful to relay in this story, Joseph was buried in Potter's field in a numbered grave. One day, we will give him a proper burial.

Early in our lives we learned that life was hard and we had to be strong, stick together, and always try to find the good in whatever situation we found ourselves in. Of course, as children we didn't think of it in such grown-up terms, but we knew that if we were to survive we would have to be able to push the feeling of pain away. Our dad was the person who kept us going. He told us that he wanted to keep his kids, but the city wouldn't let him. That's why we were sent first to a shelter and then foster homes. But, just knowing that he was there for us was enough to keep us going. The promise of one day going home and being a family was the dream we held onto.

You might ask, where was the rest of our family? All the other brothers and sisters that our mom had from relationships and marriages? Like I said before, we met them one by one. Nothing formal, they would just show up at our father's house, and Dad would introduce them. As far as grandparents go, like I said before, we only knew our dad's mom. We didn't like it when she visited at Christmas, because she was strict and made us eat things we didn't like and drink hot milk before we went to bed. She also wore a wig, and when she took it off, it scared the pee out of us!

But most of the time, the adults we were around were just plain MEAN. Being mean to kids makes them afraid, scared and lonely, so we were always afraid of something; lonely for love; and scared of the world. I remember I used to try to use my magical powers to find me and my brother and my sister a nice family. But my powers didn't really work most of the time. I just thought they didn't work when I was scared or hungry — and back then, I was ALWAYS hungry, and ALWAYS scared.

I think the only person besides us who really knew the whole story of our family was Miss Gale; she was the social worker from the foster agency who was in charge of us. At least she was the person who always came when it was time to move us to another foster home. I can see her face to this day, it was like a stone with blank eyes. I mean, she never really looked us in the eyes. It was like she looked around us, and through us, but never AT us. Her visits felt like somebody had dumped ice cubes in our underwear, and when she left, it took days before the chill left our bodies.

My real feelings about her ... well, she was like a robot without a heart!

Introduction
Our Name Isn't "Foster"
by George

The kids in our new school call us the *Foster Kids*. That would have been fine if that was our last name. But it isn't. They called us that because we lived in a foster home.

A foster home is where they place you when they take you from your real parents (or your parents don't want you anymore, or something else bad happens) and they give you to a new family. For some kids, it's great. They go from a bad home to a better one. But we were never that lucky.

With us, we kept going from one bad home to another. It was like that ever since I could remember. My sister Emma was only three years old when we got sent to our first foster home. I think that was back in like, the 1950s. Me? I was only two. My brother Joseph was a baby.

I forgot to introduce myself. My name is George. In this story I am twelve, Joseph is ten, and Emma is thirteen.

So after all these years, we've decided to tell our tale, or at least this version of it.

1

We are Stars

by George

Today is the greatest day of our lives! Our team won the *Sixth Grade Dream Gift Project!* I know that may not sound like much, but IT IS! Maybe it's because me, my brother and my sister won something for the first time in our lives. Or maybe it's because we haven't had a lot of great days. But like everything in our lives, it was an adventure!!!

It seems like everything changed for us when the Morrises became our parents. We were in a new home (a good one!), going to a new school, and for the first time that I can remember, we were happy. Really happy!

Who would have thunk it! That's my favorite phrase — I made it up. We make up a lot of stuff — it always helped us to survive when everything was so bad that we just wanted to stay in bed all day and cry. But those days were over!

Who would have believed that just a little while ago we were three lonely scared foster kids? Now we're the most popular kids in PS 206. Well, us and our team. But it just feels like it happened to only us. Even the people in the neighborhood are talking about how we won first place!

The members of our team were me, my sister Emma, my brother Joseph, our friends Cathy-Jane, Benjamin, Hector, Maria, Sam Lee, Ant and Rodney, Ant's real name is Anthony but they call him Ant because he's sooo small. He's even smaller than me, my brother and sister, and everyone talks about how skinny we are.

Well, we used to be skinnier before Mrs. Morris fattened us up. And I mean REALLY skinny. We were so thin that kids used to call us names like skinny or midgets. And some kids called us *rag-a-muffins* (because of the ugly clothes we had to wear). We all hated that! But some of the names weren't so bad; like vanilla, chocolate and strawberry. We didn't mind that since we all liked ice cream. They started calling us that because everyone said we didn't really look like brothers and sister.

Emma and I are really light skinned, and Joseph is really brown. So I was called strawberry because I have these really rosy red cheeks. Emma is vanilla, because she has almost no color in her face at all. And you guessed it, Joseph was chocolate.

But the name of our team is "The Dream Team." I named the team that because I just always knew it would take teamwork if we wanted to win the Sixth Grade Project. We had a dream and to make the dream come to life, we had to stick together!

And you know what? It must be a dream, because even Rodney, the school bully, became the nicest kid in the world once he finally joined the team. Tell you about that later. Talk about smiling, Rodney does it all the time now. But he never use to. In fact, we didn't even know he had teeth, because he just growled and frowned! Rodney doesn't even beat up kids anymore. Well, at least he hasn't beaten anyone up since we won the contest. I think that's a new record for him.

Even my sister is smiling; I mean REALLY smiling, 'cause the cutest boy in the school is taking her to the graduation picnic. It's a surprise who that boy is. (Tell you that later, too.) Yuck! But it's nice to see her so happy. I mean, she always smiled a lot before, but I know she only did it so we wouldn't feel so alone, so afraid. But now, she's smiling because she's really happy — her eyes tell me that. I got a thing for eyes — what you feel, the eyes can't hide. My dad used to say that about people.

The rest of the team must all like being stars, too. And being a STAR can really change a kid. In fact, I like how this feels so much that I want to be a star when I grow up! Like I said, *"Who would have thunk it!"*

But I should get back to the story. How did we win? How did we do it? Easy, with teamwork! Oh, and a dog named Sidney. Can't forget Sidney, the smartest dog on the entire planet. Maybe in the galaxy. Probably the whole universe and beyond!

Now don't think it was easy. It took a lot of hard work! Success always does. Most of the time, we didn't really know what we were doing, but we stuck together, and made it work. And the drama between Maria and Emma? *OMIGOSH!* Plus the nutty stuff Rodney did to try and make us fail. Even Sidney did some stuff to drive us crazy. Do you believe that dog actually ran away the morning of the second show?! But my sister Emma is the real story teller. I just wanted to say my part first, 'cause once she starts talking, I might not get a chance again. My sister LOVES to talk!

So now, I'm going to shut up and let Emma be in charge.

Emma LOVES to be in charge. Fair is fair — she deserves to be in charge because she has always taken really good care of Joseph and me.

2
On the move ...again
by Emma

My name is Emma. I'm 13, so I'm the oldest. I'm also the only girl. It's always been my job to take care of George and Joseph. I'm going to begin our adventure when we went to live with Mr. and Mrs. Morris. That's when everything started to get better. Much better!

Miss Gale, the lady from the Foster agency, said we were going to a place like the country. A place with lots of grass and trees. "But we like the city," George grumbled. "I like watching my friends play stickball from the window."

"Friends? We don't even really know those boys in our neighborhood," I said. How could we? We were hardly ever allowed to go outside to play. But when we DID get to go out, we made the most of it. George was so funny that all the kids just wanted to be around him. Besides, he was always trying to put on some type of show. Mostly magic shows. That boy could invent magic out of dirt! One time he actually made pies out of mud, and told the kids on the block that they were flying saucers from outer space. I think he invented the first Frisbee, because he would sail them hard mud pies up in the air and the kids would go nuts trying to catch them!

Buts let's get back to the move to the Morrises.

"Are we going to see any cows or horses?" Joseph asked.

"No cows. No horses. But maybe some rabbits," Miss Gale added, without even looking in Joseph's direction. A response from her was rare because she hardly ever commented on anything. Talking to her was like talking to a wall.

"I wish I could make HER disappear," George whispered under his breath. I looked at George who was glaring at Miss Gale. That means he really IS trying to make her disappear. That's because he thinks he's got magical powers. Yep, George thinks he can really make things disappear. That's because once (and only ONCE) he made a rabbit disappear from inside of a hat. Well. Not really ... but don't tell him that.

Okay, this is how it happened. It was one of those times we were actually allowed to go downstairs and play in front of our apartment building in New York City. That didn't happen too often, maybe two times a week. But ONLY if we were good and did all of our chores. George was putting on a magic show for some kids on the block. And for the grand finale he put a rabbit in this old black hat that he found in the empty lot across the street from where we lived. Not only did he find the hat, but we also found the rabbit. We called him Bubba, and kept him in the hallway in our building. You might ask how does one find a rabbit in a empty lot? You see, every spring for a couple of weeks, the empty lot became the site for this amusement park. Within days the men would turn the lot into a place filled with rides and all kinds of booths where you could buy food, and see all kinds of shows.

The amusement park was a terrific place; especially at night with all the colored lights and kids screaming on the rides: The rides that went up in the air, and twisted and turned and scared the living daylights out of you. Although we seldom had money to go on the rides, we would hang out at the park, just enjoying the sights and the smells of food coming from the booths. It was one of the few times that our foster mother would let us stay out at night. The world was safer then, and kids stayed out even after dark, sat on the stoop, and played with their friends. But George, he was fascinated by the man who did magic tricks. That's where he must have gotten the idea to become a magician!

When the fair ended, we would all search the lot for loose change, and empty soda bottles to cash in for two cents a bottle at the local candy store. We all waited for that, because a kid could sometimes make as much as 25 cents on those days. That was big money back then. One day when we were looking for bottles, George found this rabbit, and named it Bubba. We kept him in the hallway, and all the kids on the block helped us feed him — mostly lettuce from the local grocer. Mr. Joe, the man who ran the store was a nice man, and after we showed him Bubba, he always saved stuff for us. For free!

After George found that rabbit, and the hat, he started putting on his own magic shows. He would put an old towel around his shoulders, said it was his cape, put on that black hat, and made a wand from a stick. That was his official magician's outfit. The grand finale was always to try and make Bubba disappear. But it never worked, because the rabbit would simply crawl out of the hat and sit on the old box that George had set up as his magician's stand. But this one day, something happened that convinced George, and all the kids who were standing around, that he was truly a magician. He put Bubba in the hat, and yelled, "abbra cadabra," and waved his wand.

Suddenly, a car from across the street backfired. Those old cars used to do that a lot. Not sure why, but all of a sudden you'd hear a big Boom! Then a puff of smoke would come out the tailpipe. It scared the heck out of all of us, especially George and Joseph because they didn't like loud noises. And it scared Bubba, too, because when all the kids turned around to see where the sound was coming from, he jumped out the hat ran for his life. I was the only one who saw it make a beeline for the empty lot.

When the kids turned back around, that rabbit was nowhere to be seen. Of course, everyone THOUGHT that George had really made Bubba disappear. He was so happy that I didn't have the heart to tell him the truth. From that day on, George thought he had some type of magical powers, and that's what he told everybody. In fact, he was so convinced of his powers, that he never let that black hat out of his sight. He carried that stinky ol' hat with him to every foster home we lived in. I guess he hoped that one day Bubba would pop out, but obviously that never happened.

Even though he missed him, George felt so good about being able to make that rabbit disappear, that he promised me and Joseph that he would use his powers to find us a really nice family — A family that would keep us and not send us back to the shelter. I loved my brother for believing that he would find us a home. You see, George had that cheery, *dream-the-impossible-dream* way about him. He could get happy just watching snow fall, but Joseph and I were different. We were kind of skeptics, in other words, we had lost hope in ever being placed with a nice family. And since I was the oldest, it was my job to look out for my brothers; and magic was not going to make that happen as far as I was concerned.

Soon after George declared that he had magical powers, all of a sudden Joseph declared that he was a superhero. That's right, a superhero. Don't laugh. Like I said, we had to do anything we could to make our lives bearable. Joseph said he realized he had powers also 'cause one day in school, some kids tripped him on the stairs, but instead of falling, he just rolled down the steps. When he landed, he just lay there. Real still. Everyone thought he was dead! I think HE even thought he was dead because he said he just stayed on the floor for at least five minutes before he got up! By that time there was a crowd, and everyone was really scared that something awful had happened to him. But when the school nurse came, he jumped right up! The principal said that a fall like that could have broken all the bones in Joseph's body. It was a miracle; he didn't even have a bloody nose … a scratch … nothing!

When we got home from school that day, we started calling him Superman. Joseph loved that! So he took an old shirt and painted the Superman emblem on the front. Unfortunately, he made the "S" backwards. He always does that — makes some of his letters and numbers backwards. But he still loved that shirt. In fact, unless the shirt is being washed, he has it on! That night he told George and me that when he started falling down the steps, it felt like somebody was holding him up and then gently placed him at the bottom of the stairs. The feeling was so awesome, that he couldn't move. You know what I think? I think it was an ANGEL!

To this day, it's still his favorite shirt. I know it's old and too small for him now, but it's still his favorite thing to wear. Of course, I know he doesn't have super powers, but I ain't never going to tell him, just like I ain't never gonna tell George about his "fake" magical powers. I know it sounds silly, but I never want to burst their bubbles. Hey, a kid's gotta have something to believe in. Right? Wish I did.

Me? I don't have any special powers and I like I said, I sure don't believe in magic. In fact, except for what happened to Joseph, I don't believe in much of anything like that. I stopped believing that good things would ever happen for us the day that Miss Gale told me how hard it would be to find a family that would keep us. You know, a real family like the ones other kids have, or like the happy families you see on TV. Yep. Miss Gale told me, "Most people don't want three kids because they're just too much trouble." It hurt me to hear her say that no one would want us. But that's how she was. Nobody should ever tell a kid something like that — it's just plain MEAN! Some people act like kids don't have feelings. But we do!

Mean or not, Miss Gale was right, and we did change homes a LOT! I guess at first people THINK they can handle three kids, and they want that money; but they soon realize they can't. It's not that we're noisy and break stuff. Probably no more than other kids. And it's definitely not 'cause we eat a lot. It's just the opposite. In fact, you can actually see Joseph's ribs, he looks like a skeleton! Plus George is shorter than a poodle. Even me, I'm very petite for my age. Petite is a nice way to say small. It's so embarrassing, and although I'm a thirteen-year-old girl, I still wear boys' undershirts. Know what I mean?

But I guess it's that taking care of three kids that aren't yours is just too much to ask. Not even the money made folks keep us for long. But worse than being sent back to the shelter, the families that took us in never even tried to love us. Never treated us nice. But at least we got to stay together. Our daddy made sure of that! No matter what happened, he always insisted that we not be separated. The same for my three older brothers, Walter, Edward and Scottie, they always stayed together. I wish we could ALL be together, but let's face it, don't NOBODY want to take in SIX kids!

Like I told you before, as the oldest, it was my job to watch out for my brothers. They needed me to protect them from all the awful things that could happen to kids like us. Even the *hardly-ever-speaks-to-us* Miss Gale told me, "Emma, teach your brothers to be quiet. And don't complain or you kids will have to go back to the shelter." I know we mentioned the shelter before, but did we tell you what it is? Well, the shelter was this awful place where kids who have no home would be sent until somebody wanted them. Shelters are dark, cold places. I remember we were in this large room with rows of beds. The blankets were brown, and the metal bed frames were old and painted gray. And if you laid down too fast you'd hit your head on the frame, and boy would it hurt!

Thank goodness we had a daddy who loved us and who came to see us. When I was older he told me that when he would leave he could hear me crying and screaming. It made him want to cry, too. George would just sit and sing to himself. Like I said, he was one cheerful kid. I do remember that when I would start to cry the people in the shelter would say to me, "if you don't stop crying we're gonna put you in the basement." That's when I learned to be quiet and just wait for our daddy to come back.

The people in those places ain't nice, always yelling and threatening to put you by yourself in the basement. Don't know what was in the basement, but it wasn't a place I wanted to be sent to. So I made sure that George and I were quiet as church mice. Joseph, was in another part of the building. We seldom got to see him. I think it was because he was just a little baby and we were bigger. Don't know what would have happened to us if it were not for our dad. But I can imagine …

3

Mr. and Mrs. Morris
by Emma

It was a long ride from the city to our new home. We must have stopped a hundred times for George to go to the bathroom. He peed a lot! Unfortunately most times it was in the bed. Once we got off the main road, it still took us a while to get to the house. Finally, we turned down a dirt road and saw the house in the distance. As we got closer, we saw the front door open and a man and a woman came out to meet us. Miss Gale turned off the engine and opened the doors to let us out. But none of us were in a hurry. Why rush, we'll probably only be here for a few weeks before they send us back anyway.

"C'mon, children," said Miss Gale. "I'd like to introduce you to Mr. and Mrs. Morris."

I sighed, then got out the car. My brothers followed. Then Miss Gale led us to the house where we walked up the three stairs to the porch. There we were, getting ready to meet our "parents" for the first time. I think this will be our fourth ... no, fifth foster home. They looked at us. We looked at them. Nobody said a word.

Then Joseph took his two fingers out of his mouth (he sucked them all the time) and said, "Wow, you're really old!" I felt my heart stop. It was true, they were old, but still, that's not the first thing you want your new parents to hear. Joseph doesn't talk a lot, but then when he does, oh boy, it usually meant trouble!

You see, Joseph, although very quiet, had a sad way about him. Daddy told us that he had been born after our mother had been hospitalized, and she hardly ever got to hold him, so he never really got to know our mother. I guess that affects the way a kid sees the world. I guess stuff like no love, no cuddles, no "mama time" can make a kid weird. After he said that, I started to turn around and walk back to the car, but Miss Gale, in her usual robot style, began to talk.

"Mr. and Mrs. Morris, these are the Fraser children: Emma, George, and that little rascal there is Joseph."

Mrs. Morris, was a short fat lady, with gray hair. She had an apron on, a blue dress with flowers, and these funny looking black shoes. Mr. Morris, was also fat, with gray hair — but he was tall, so he didn't look so round. Dressed in black pants and a plaid shirt, he looked like one of those men who put together the rides for the amusement park. I don't know why, but I liked the Morrises from the moment I saw them. Maybe because they were both smiling and seemed to be happy to meet us. Now that was something that had never happened when we went to new homes. Most times, those people just looked at us with blank eyes (like Miss Gale). It was like we were packages that the mailman just dropped off instead of little kids. One time when we got dropped off to our new home, they just stood us in the living room and told us that if we acted bad, they would send us back immediately. And they did! Even though we were good and did everything they told us to do. Go figure.

Mr. Morris just stood quietly and smiled. But Mrs. Morris threw open her arms and said, "Welcome to your new home, children, we've been waiting for you. Now come here and let me hug you *cutie pies*! Bill, go to the car and get the rest of their bags."

I was watching the man she called Bill. He had a kind face, and eyes that seemed to glow. I liked him. He started towards the car. I thought to myself, nobody ever smiled at us like that before. I looked at my brothers, they looked scared. I know I was. What was he up to?

"No, I'm afraid this is it," said Miss Gale handing Mr. Morris our beat-up ol' suitcase. It had belonged to our real mother. Guess I was wrong when I said we had nothing to call our own. I always made sure that no one took that suitcase from us. So here's the deal: George had his hat, Joseph had his shirt, and I had our mother's suitcase. (Years later, when we were all grown up, we each took turns keeping it. Inside we kept George's hat, Joseph's Superman shirt, and the trophies from the Sixth Grade Project. Of course, we had a picture of Sidney our dog. Tell you more about him later.)

"Only one bag?" asked Mrs. Morris with her hand over her mouth. "For the THREE of them?"

"Yes, ma'am," I said, "we don't need a lot," and I put a big smile on my face. Smiling makes adults think we're happy little kids. But I knew from experience, that when you've been to as many foster homes as we have, you better know exactly what to say and how to act.

"We don't need much."

"We don't eat much."

"We are good at doing stuff around the house."

Folks seemed to like kids who could do stuff, didn't need anything, and were quiet.

Miss Gale told me, "Do what I tell you and maybe somebody will keep you kids." So far, no luck. ... Would life with the Morrises be different I wondered? ... Probably not!

The inside of the house was nice and clean. Not much furniture, but very clean. I liked that. And it smelled good. Really good. Like cookies. Whenever we went into a new place, we each looked for different things. Joseph looked for a TV. Not many folks had them back then. George looked for a dog. But me, I looked for stuff like beer cans, ash trays, books, pictures of family ... if I saw no pictures, I knew they were not *gonna* keep us for long. People with no photographs were usually the MEANEST of the mean. They would get rid of a kid in a blink of the eye.

"No TV!" whispered Joseph. "How are we *gonna* watch Superman?"

"And no dog!" said George. But the good thing is that there were also no ash trays or beer cans either. To me that was more important than a TV or stupid *ol'* dog. Plus, they had a whole bookcase filled with books and photographs. And some of them were of kids. Those were two real good signs. If they read a lot then maybe they wouldn't have time to watch everything we did. Less watching could mean less spankings. Yep, reading can be a really a good thing.

Miss Gale, gave us one of her blank stares, and said good bye. She told the Morrises that she would stop by in a week or so to see how we were doing. We were so scared. Then she just turned and left. We were on our own. Again. We all watched her leave. Then I turned and looked around some more. I saw more photographs of people and people with kids. This was good. Maybe, just maybe, they actually liked kids. I looked at Mrs. Morris, pointed to the photos and asked, "so, are those your kids, ma'am?"

"No," she answered. Those are my nieces and nephews. And your new cousins. We'll have to take you to meet them. We visit Aunt Hattie and Uncle Ed almost every weekend.

"Ain't you got your own kids," asked Joseph.

"No, dear. The Lord never blessed Mr. Morris and me with children of our own."

Wow, I thought to myself, she thinks that having kids is a blessing!

"Now, who wants cookies and milk?" asked Mrs. Morris, breaking the silence. We stood there unable to answer. I had taught my brothers some rules about how to act, and Rule #1 was try not to appear greedy or hungry.

"I baked them myself," she said. "Let's go into the kitchen."

We were so hungry that we forgot the rule and followed her to the door at the far side of the living room. Them cookies were amazing! Warm and gooey, filled with chocolate and crunchy nuts. Can I tell you something? We never had fresh-baked cookies before.

We saw them in TV commercials, but never in real life. Oh the smell of Mrs. Morris's cookies! Amazing!

After we finished eating those amazing cookies, they took us upstairs to show us where we'd be sleeping. The room was really nice. It was blue and had a set of wooden bunk beds, and a great big desk.

Joseph yelled out, "I get the top bunk!"

"No, dear," said Mrs. Morris, "your older brother gets the top bunk, because it's up high and you are too small. We wouldn't want you to fall and hurt yourself."

"*Awww*, I really wanted the top bed," Joseph muttered. "George pees the bed and I don't wanna be under THAT!"

I was horrified!!! Now they will surely get rid of us — a kid who pees the bed ain't wonderful. I held my breath ... waiting ... but Mrs. Morris, didn't say a word.

"*C'mon*, Joseph, we get the bottom bunk, that's fair," I said trying to show how grateful we were.

"No, Emma," said Mrs. Morris.

Uh-oh, I thought to myself. Because of Joseph's big mouth, they're probably going to make us sleep in the barn now.

Mrs. Morris continued, "This room is for your brothers. You have your OWN room," she said.

I rubbed my eyes, and slapped my ears with both hands, 'cause they must not be working right. Did she just say, "I have MY OWN room?" Yes! I had my very own room for the first time ever!!!

"I do?" I asked in shock.

"Oh yes, a young lady needs her privacy," she said.

Lady? Me? Wow!

She walked across the hall. I followed — my heart beating like a drum. I couldn't wait to see it. When she opened the door, it was like Christmas! I mean, it felt just like when we spend Christmas with our dad. The room was green with a nice big bed, a small window, and it even had a desk. I sat down on the bed to feel what it was like. I actually bounced. Was it ever soft and comfy! Some of the beds we've had to sleep in have been hard as boards. And lots of times we've had to sleep on old lumpy cots, or the floor!

After I checked out my room, I ran back to my brothers' room. Sure, theirs was nice, but mine was even was nicer! Mrs. Morris told us that she was going to take us shopping next week so that we could pick out whatever curtains and bedspreads we wanted. We just stood there speechless. We never had a bedspread. To be honest, we didn't even know what a bedspread was. But it sounded fancy, so it had to be good, right? Warm cookies, rooms of our own, bedspreads, curtains; was this what a real home felt like? My heart was still beating so fast, I thought it would pop out of my blouse! It was the first time in years that I thought maybe, just maybe, we had found a real home. Now that's a word we hardly ever said out loud. HOME.

I whispered to George, "PLEASE try not to pee the bed this time!" But Mrs. Morris heard me.

I didn't mean for her to hear, so I tried to think of something to say so they wouldn't be mad and make us sleep on the floor.

"But don't worry, George hasn't wet the bed in a while. And even then, it's only sometimes," I said smiling at her. That was not the truth. George peed the bed every single night! But I was trying to make it okay. "He only pees when he's nervous, hungry, cold or afraid. You know, like that."

George was so embarrassed he blurted out, "Well Emma sucks her thumb! Look at it! It looks like an old wrinkled bone."

I shot him a mean look and he stared down at the floor and mumbled, "Don't make me make you disappear, big sister, because you know I can."

"Well, we'll just have to work on that together, won't we?" she said while putting her hand on George's shoulder. Then she said these exact words, "Emma, all children have things they outgrow.

So not to worry, because if that's the reason your brother pees the bed or you suck your thumb, then he'll stop soon, because you kids will never be cold, hungry, nervous or afraid in this home."

I nearly peed in my own pants when she said that. Surely we must be dreaming. Don't you think?

Joseph took his two fingers out of his mouth to say something. But I shot him an even meaner look than I gave to George so he put them back in his mouth and said nothing. I didn't know what he was about to say, but I didn't want him to ruin everything.

Mrs. Morris kissed each of us and gave us the tightest hug we had ever had. For the first time in my life, I cried because I was so happy. Mrs. Morris, pretended not to see my tears. George and Joseph were just as shocked. They had never seen me cry. I was the strong one, remember? I think it scared them. I know it scared me.

"My own room," the words sounded funny inside my head. A room of MY OWN. Even if they sent us back, I would never forget how special I felt. How special we all felt. Then Mrs. Morris left. We just stood there trying to get a grip on our feelings.

After a few minutes, Mr. Morris came into the room with some towels and wash cloths. "These are for your brothers, and these are for you. Mama said girls like pink. You kids have had a long ride so you must be tired. The bathroom is down the hall, you can take a bath, and Mama will call you when supper is ready." Then he gave us a hug, too, and left the room humming a song. A MAN who gives hugs? This place was weird. Nice … but weird.

"Mama?" I thought to myself. After they left, Joseph said "I like them. They're different colors like us."

"I like them too," added George.

"We'll see," I thought.

Any moment I just knew I would wake up. Mama? Mr. Morris called her Mama. I hadn't heard that word in a long time. I whispered to my brothers, "Remember, we don't call foster folks Mama or Daddy. We just don't! That's Rule #2!"

4

Fittin' In
by Emma

During the next few months we got settled into our new home and our new school — PS 206. Those first few weeks were tough. We just didn't seem to fit in. The kids teased us, especially this kid named Rodney. He was the one that started calling us the vanilla, chocolate and strawberry kids from outer-space. I guess it was because, when kids asked were we came from we just shrugged and said nothing. Telling them that we had been in different homes was too hard to explain. Now how that meant we were from outer space is beyond me. And I already told you about the vanilla, chocolate and strawberry part.

Rodney was such a mean kid. He wasn't bad looking, but he was just so mean that no one ever wanted to be around him. PLUS he smelled really bad. His clothes were old and too small for his big body. And just because he was bigger than most of the other kids, he bullied everyone, not just us. But since we were really small for our ages, and we were new, he really seemed to focus on making our lives a nightmare. But despite his bullying, we eventually made some friends. We liked this kid named "Ant" because he would try to help us when Rodney would start his name calling. Now Ant was even smaller than us, but he was brave. And though Rodney would laugh at him, he'd usually stop teasing us. How could that big bully be afraid of such a small peanut of a kid? Go figure. I guess size don't really matter if you have guts. Ant became George's *bestest* friend.

Now school work was easy for me and my brothers since we all liked to read. That's what happens when you're bored and never really had any toys or friends to play with. Sometimes we were allowed to watch television, but not often. Most times the foster homes didn't even have TVs, so all we had was each other and our school books. So we played school a lot, and of course I was the teacher. Our dad always told us how important it was to be good readers, too. Probably because he wasn't really a strong reader himself and knew how that affected his life. Mr. and Mrs. Morris were surprised when they got our first report cards. I guess they thought that being foster kids automatically meant that we weren't smart. You should have seen the surprise on their faces once they saw all the A's we got. Of course I got the most. Mr. Morris checked the names to make sure they were really our report cards. We even surprised our teachers!

Soon we all started to make other friends and things were starting to get good. Really good! Except for Rodney. But Ant kept him in check as best as he could. To us he was *Ant-the-mighty-warrior-and-champion-of-the-universe.*

Every morning we ate breakfast in the kitchen with Mr. and Mrs. Morris. It was nice to be with people who actually LIKED to see us eat. Especially Mrs. Morris! She'd put more food on our plates before we even finished what she had already given us. Shoot, in one of them other foster homes, I forget which one, they used to have a lock on the refrigerator so we couldn't get food. A LOCK! No lie!

I didn't want to tell you this, but sometimes in those other homes, we were so hungry that we stole food from the supermarket. George was really good at it, being so cute, with all that curly hair and rosy red cheeks. He always took Joseph with him. He would sneak off the block and go to the Safeway Supermarket. No one ever seemed to suspect them. But, despite my careful instructions about what to take, (stuff that's good for you like fruit and crackers) George always stole candy. Lots of candy. That's why we all had terrible teeth and lots of cavities. Never could figure out why the foster agency didn't figure out why we were so skinny but had such bad teeth. Couldn't figure out why they didn't see the bruises from the spankings, either. I guess grown folks see what grown folks want to see.

Yep, all those folks at that agency must have been trained to see only what they wanted to see. Oh well, it was part of my responsibility as the oldest to feed my brothers. I was the organizer. A full stomach was worth the pain of the dentist drill. That's what I always told George and Joseph. Not that any of those people ever took us to the dentist either. The LAST thing that any of them wanted to do was to spend money on US!

Now in our new home, we ate our stomachs full every day. But even though we had all the food we wanted, George and Joseph STILL kept sneaking rolls off the table and putting them in their pockets so they'll have something to eat later. We had done that for years because we had too, and we just didn't really believe that the Morrises were going to keep feeding us. Guess we were waiting for them to put a chain lock around their refrigerator, too.

I tried to stop them from hiding food, but nothing I said worked.

"She LIKES to feed us," I kept telling them, but they always kept a stash. I didn't try too hard, though, because deep down I couldn't blame them.

Mrs. Morris would always say, "I have to fatten you three up. You children are skinny as rails." And she meant it. We were getting fatter and fatter, and to my surprise, I had to trade in my undershirts for my first bra. Now you get what I was trying to tell you before. It's hard to say 'cause it's embarrassing. But now you know.

George and Joseph teased me, "Emma's got a bra that looks like a band aid." No matter, I was one happy camper, and I made sure that my bra strap was always sticking outside my blouse. You know, like hanging on my arm, below my shirt sleeve? Hey, what's the fun of wearing your first bra if nobody knows it?

Although things were the best ever, I didn't like what was happening to my brothers. They absolutely loved Mr. and Mrs. Morris. Several times, I heard them slip and call them mom and dad. But, the rule was, we don't call foster people mom and dad. No, sir! Besides, we still had a daddy and a mother. Our REAL parents.

And even though George and Joseph had that look in their eyes — that sad look from always having to say, "Yes, sir," or "Yes, ma'am" instead of, "Okay, mommy and daddy." I warned them not to get attached to these people. Sure, I knew, that just like me, they had been waiting to call someone mommy and daddy their whole lives. Not just those few times a year when we got to see our real parents. It was especially hard when it came to our mother since we hardly ever got to see her. And to tell you the truth, when we did see her, we never called her Mom, we just sort of said, "Hi." Nevertheless, they'd better not break the rule. Sometimes, I felt so mean, reminding them to call the Morrises Mr. and Mrs., instead of mom and dad; but I've got to watch out for my brothers. It was my job. Always has been, and until things changed, if ever, I was gonna take care of us. Kids' hearts can get broken from trying to make folks their parents; especially folks who don't really want them. That's how it has always been so why should I believe that it would be different now?

Trust me, it's better this way because if we have to go back to the shelter, the Morrises won't be nothing more than some folks we called Mr. and Mrs. I learned that a long time ago. It's called survival. Keep it simple, no tears, and no real good-byes. We all knew the drill. Miss Gale would come, tell us we were moving and to pack our suitcase. Then we would run quickly to the car before anyone could see the tears in our eyes. We can't take that chance. Call them Mommy and Daddy — NO, way! Not even the Morrises — the nicest people in the whole world — so far. ...

I remember in one of them foster homes, during the summer, when school was out, they would lock us in a room all day, and fed us hominy grits for every meal. You ever had grits? They're good if you fix 'em with butter and salt. But we had to eat them plain. Then they taste like saw dust. *Yuck!*

We were always scared and hungry in those other places. That had to be why we were all so weird compared to other kids. You know, George peeing the bed every night, Joseph sucking his middle fingers, and me sucking my thumb? The dentist told my daddy that because I sucked my thumb, that was why my front top teeth stuck out, and I sort of looked like that rabbit George had found in the lot. Bubba.

But even when folks were mean to us, we still tried to be good so they wouldn't send us back. Because we knew from experience, that the next place might even be worse! So, we always did our chores, took out the garbage, made our beds and did whatever they told us to do. Most of all we pretended we weren't hungry, even when we were, and we never asked for anything. But no matter what, it never worked. Then Miss Gale would come for a visit, walk around, pat us on the head like puppies, and tell us to pack our bag "because we were moving." Of course, as the oldest, I would ask Why? But I already knew.

Miss Gale would just look down at me with those blank zombie eyes and say, "Three kids are too much to handle so they're sending you back." A couple of times I wanted to ask her, "did they tell you that they hit us, and starved us?" But I never told her any of those things. It wouldn't have done any good anyway. I knew that. Sometimes I just wanted to scream.

We never told her any of the bad stuff. I even told George and Joseph not to tell. Don't know why, I think because somehow I felt it was our fault. Maybe if we tried harder somebody would love us, want us, or just keep us for longer than a blink. We were just some kids who wanted to borrow a mommy and daddy until ours could take us back.

But, it was not all bad. There was Christmas! It was the happiest time of the year for us. Our real father would come and take us to his house for three whole days. He lived in Brooklyn. We also got to be with our three older brothers. Walter, Edward and Scottie were lucky 'cause they got to stay in one home for their whole life. I was happy for them, and a little bit jealous. Okay, a LOT jealous! So I'm not going to talk about them. Just that we loved being with them and the world was a beautiful place when we were all together as a family at Christmas time.

Let me get back to Christmas with our Dad. Since I was the only girl, he would take me shopping with him for the food. I got to pick anything I wanted! My favorite food was Wonder Bread! I used to ball up a slice and stuff the whole thing in my mouth. It took three shopping carts to carry all the food that daddy bought. And it was all just for us. My daddy must have known how hungry we were, because we ate all day and into the night. We even took food to bed. Daddy never said a word. See why we loved him so much?

Selecting the Christmas tree was super fun. Daddy would wait until the day before Christmas, and buy the biggest tree he could find. Sometimes it cost as much as **$4.00!** That was a lot of money for a Christmas tree. Then we would all decorate it, and eat and eat and eat. Plus we got to stay up late to watch our favorite movie on his big black and white television: "A Christmas Carol."

You know, that movie with Mr. Scrooge and Tiny Tim? I really liked the part when The Ghost of Christmas Past came and made Mr. Scrooge realize how mean he had been to Tiny Tim. Wish that would happen to Rodney, you know, the bully from my school? My brothers and I wished that time would stand still because we didn't ever want our visit to end. But it did, and back we would go to the foster home. But from the day that daddy took us back, we started counting down the days to NEXT Christmas. We kept a calendar hidden in our suitcase, and every night before bedtime, we would cross off a day. *OMIGOSH!* 365 days is a long time when you're waiting for something special.

All that changed when we went to live with the Morrises. Daddy told us that the Morrises told him that he could visit us as often as he could. So we got to see our Daddy more than ever now. Can you imagine, they liked us, AND they liked our daddy? In the other homes, we hardly ever saw him. Shoot, those other people probably didn't want him to know how bad they treated us. But just before our first Christmas with the Morrises, Daddy told us that he had to work (he was a cab driver) and couldn't take us home that year. I guess he needed the money to pay for all that food he bought the last time we stayed with him. We were heartbroken! Imagine waiting a whole year for something only to find out that it wasn't going to happen. But Daddy and the Morrises promised that they would make our Christmas super special. We still cried at the thought of not being with him. But at least we were in a nice home. Something weird happened to me after that, I got scared and I started to wonder if the Morrises were trying to take us from our daddy. But I have to admit, when Christmas came, it was special, just like Daddy told us it would be.

Mrs. Morris made pies and cakes, and cooked a big turkey. And Mr. Morris took us to New York City to see the tree at Rockefeller Center. It was the biggest Christmas tree that any of us had ever seen! Then he took us to this store called Macy's that we had seen in this movie called Miracle on 34th Street. We didn't even know that it was a real store!!! They decorated all the windows with toys and Christmas scenes. We stood in front of the windows for hours just looking and *oohing*.

The real treat was when we got to meet Santa and sit on his lap! You know what always puzzled me about Santa Claus? He was always white. I wondered about that, since we were colored, even though George and I looked white, (or so we heard folks say). But Joseph, he was brown. I guess George and I would have been happy with a white Santa, but it was Joseph who asked me, "Emma, how come Santa ain't brown like me? I made up some story about Santa living in the North Pole, where it was very cold, and he had to stay indoors to keep warm, so he never had enough sun to turn him brown. Joseph, just looked at me, and mumbled something under his breath. I heard it, but I pretended I didn't. You know what my little brother mumbled?

"When I grow up, I'm going to be the first brown Santa, so kids that look like me don't feel bad about being brown." I guess I never realized that Joseph felt like an outsider because George and I were light, and he was darker. I never realized it until then.

On those trips to the city, Mr. Morris even bought us hot chocolate and gingerbread men. I always ate mine the same way. First, the head. Then the legs. Then the arms. But George and Joseph swallowed theirs in like two bites. Not me, I wanted to make mine last. On Christmas Eve, Mrs. Morris read us *Twas the Night Before Christmas*. OMIGOSH! We went to bed some happy kids. The only thing that would have made the day better is if Daddy and our brothers could have been with us. But it was still LOTS of fun!

But the biggest surprise were the gifts we got on Christmas day. We each got a toy that Daddy had sent us, and some new clothes from Mr. and Mrs. Morris. George got a magic game, and Joseph got an entire Superman outfit, including the cape. Me? I got the prettiest red dress I have ever seen. We gave the Morrises a card that we made all by ourselves. They acted like we gave them a gift that cost a hundred dollars. But it was just a card we made using the funnies from the Sunday paper. Of course they gave us hugs. They used any excuse to hug us. It was always hug time in the Morris house. We just loved it! Gradually, we started hugging them back, and they loved our hugs just as much as we loved theirs.

The Morrises hugged us every time they saw us. Never really had so many hugs or gifts like that before from foster people. One time, I remember that we lived with these people who wrapped empty boxes and put them under the tree. *Ain't* NO fun in opening an empty box. Why would anyone do that? Like I told you, some folks are just MEAN!!!!

On New Year's Eve we stayed up til midnight! We ate pie and drank hot cider. I must have gained five pounds during the holidays. This was great because George and Joseph had to finally stop teasing me since I was finally filling out my bra. After the holidays, when we went back to school, everyone said we were glowing! Whatever that meant.

5

6th Grade Project
by Emma

Well now that you know all about us, I guess it's time I told you about the Sixth Grade Project. You know, the one that made us famous? Although it was a project, all the kids said it was a contest, because we had to compete against each other, and only one team could be the winner! And that team was us! The Dream Team. We won. Yes we did!

Every morning, the three of us walked to school with Hector, he was one of our new best friends. But one morning, by the time Hector got to our house, he was already out of breath.

"Sam Lee told Maria and she told me that Rodney "the Beast" is on the loose!" he said huffing and puffing.

That's all we needed to hear. We immediately scooted out the door. Hector was so scared he could hardly speak, "Come on, you guys, we've got to get to school early!" he said still gasping for air. He had run the entire three roads to our house. Our neighborhood was pretty with green lawns and most houses had a picket fence out front and long driveways. But there were also huge empty lots with grass and bushes. Not like the lots in city that were dirty and yucky. Mr. Morris told us that we lived in Queens.

Now, our school was huge and lots of kids went there. But unlike the city, where we had always lived before, the school was only two stories high, with a big front lawn and a big yard for the kids to play in. The yard had swings, a see-saw, and monkey bars. All the boys would climb the monkey bars and swing from the metal railings. The girls mostly used the swings and see-saw, or stayed in groups pretending not to looks at the boys.

But anyway, back to Rodney. Ant and C J (that's Cathy-Jane) were running up the path to our house, too. Ant lived down the road from us, and C J lived around the corner. We could tell by the looks on their faces that they already knew about Rodney. We grabbed our stuff and the six of us all hurried on our way. By the time we got to school, we were ALL huffing and puffing. We arrived just in time to see Rodney entering the schoolyard.

And as soon as the rest of the kids spotted him: **STAMPEDE!!!**

Everyone ran like they were zebras running from a lion. Like they were running for their lives. And they probably were. By the time the bell rang, the yard was completely empty.

We entered the school, looked around to see if Rodney was hanging out in the hallway, then headed to our class. C J , Ant and I nearly ran over our teacher, Miss Dollywog getting to our seats. Rodney came in a few minutes later, grooving to his transistor radio. (Those were the first radios that you could take with you and carry in one hand because they used batteries instead of electricity. You didn't even have to plug them into a wall socket.) You see, not only was Rodney a *cotton-picking* bully, but he was a music freak. Rodney was always whistling a song or singing something. That boy could almost repeat the words of every song in the universe. But he never passed a single test in school. Most kids said that he couldn't read.

Rodney showed us his knuckles and said, "Next time you won't be so lucky! If I catch you in the yard, I'm gonna punch your eyes out!"

Punch our eyes out? Can he even DO that? We just looked at Rodney, and Ant stuck out his tongue. Was he crazy?! I wondered what Ant wanted to be buried in 'cause Rodney was going to beat him to a pulp for that. But before Rodney could say something else to Ant, we heard the static of the loud speaker.

"Good morning. This is Principal Johnson. I'd like to wish you all a HAPPY NEW YEAR! I hope you had a wonderful holiday vacation. I have exciting news for you all. Once again it's time for the annual Sixth Grade Dream Gift Project. Your mission is to come up with a way to raise enough money to buy a gift for every child in the Special Care Unit at Hope Hospital.

"The success of the Project is up to each of you. The winning team will be announced at the Awards Assembly on May 25th. At the conclusion of this announcement, your teachers will tell you more about it."

Everyone in the class starting talking. This was an annual event for the school, and everyone was looking forward to it.

"Children, quiet down," said Miss Dollywog. "I know you are excited."

Miss Dollywog began to read us the rules while Maria handed out copies to each of us.

All Teams must do the following:

- *Elect a Team Leader and officers; everyone on the team must participate.*
- *Create a project to raise funds.*
- *Prepare a budget of how much money you will need to do your project.*
- *Teams may select other kids from the fourth, and fifth grade to join their team.*
- *Teams must submit a plan for their project by April 10th.*

Rodney crumbled his list up, threw it on the floor and went back to listening to the radio he says he got for Christmas. But some of the kids said he stole it, since it was known that Rodney lived where the really poor people lived. And he smelled like rotten eggs. Always. *Yuck!*

Ant asked the question we all wanted to ask, but were afraid to, "Miss Dollywog, does everyone have to be on a team?"

"Yes, everyone in the sixth grade must be on a team. That's why we have been working in groups all year. You now know how to work in teams and what it takes to be successful as a group. Every member of the team must cooperate and contribute. After lunch, I will give you your team assignments."

That meant Rodney was going to be on a team. Picture that!

"Wait a minute!" C J yelled out, Don't we get to pick who we want on our team?"

"Yes and no!" Miss Dollywog replied. "I'll pick some and you'll pick some. Remember this: In life, you will not always have the opportunity to pick who you will work with or who will be in your group."

"But this isn't life, this is school!" CJ grumbled.

"No fair!" the whole class yelled. "We want to be with our friends!"

"Settle down, class, it's time to begin today's lessons," said Miss Dollywog, who was starting to get impatient.

At lunch, all the kids were talking about the project. Everyone was anxious to see who was going to be on their team. "Hope we're on the same team, Emma," said Ant.

Hector laughed and yelled, "Anthony-the-Ant likes Emma."

But Ant gave it right back to him. "Shut up, you peanut head," he said, "You like CJ!"

Hector loved to tease Ant about stuff like his height, the size of his head … you name it. But Ant didn't mind, because inside his big head, he claimed to have a really big brain. He knew that for sure, because he was good in math. In fact, he was a genius in math. He got 100 on every math test.

Ant even had his very own bank account, and he carried his bank book around with him all the time. Once he showed us the amount — he had $3.15!

After lunch, we all rushed back to our class to see our team assignments. Miss Dollywog had written them on the chalk board. There were four teams from our class: Team A, Team B, Team C and Team D. Three of them were lucky. One was not. Take a look:

Team A	Team B	Team C	Team D
George	Marina	Anthony	Anna
Ian	Clay	Cathy-Jane	Michael
Nate	Scout	Maria	Aren
Seve	Oliver	Emma	Lila
Gabriel	Jaylen	Sam Lee	Chase
Blake	Catherine	Rodney	Elizabeth
Ezra	Dana		Suzy

Rodney "the bully," was on my team!!! This was the worst news ever. Everyone on the team just looked at one another; you could see the fear in our eyes. Ant whispered: "Team C" must mean we are on the "Crazy Team."

"Children," said Miss Dollywog, "Please find your team members, review the rules, and start discussing your ideas for the team project."

Then out of nowhere, a howl-like scream came from the back of the room. It scared the whole class. Even Miss Dollywog looked startled. We all froze. Rodney jumped from his chair and shouted! "I'm NOT going to be on any stupid ol' team! And you can't make me!"

"SIT DOWN, young man!" yelled Miss Dollywog with the veins in her head popping out. Rodney had that effect on most folks. But he didn't sit down. Instead, he shoved his desk aside, which sent his books flying.

"I'm not going to do this. NO! NEVER! NOT EVER!" he growled.

Wow! That was weird, even for HIM!

"Its okay, Rodney," said some of the kids in the class trying to calm him down. But "it was better than okay" I thought to myself. This could be the answer to all of our prayers since nobody in the class wanted "the bully" on their team. Rodney already had a bad reputation, that he earned every bit of, 'cause at one time or another, he had tried to beat up almost every kid in the school. And anyone who had escaped his clutches knew it was just a matter of time before **POW! BAM! SPLAT!**

"That's it! You are out of this class, young man!" Miss Dollywog screamed. Boy, her eyeballs were bulging like jawbreakers.

"Fine!" he snapped. Then Rodney bolted for the door and disappeared.

"Yea!!!" the whole class cheered — But only after we were sure he couldn't hear us.

It took a few minutes for us to settle down. Then we got into our teams.

Whew! Rodney was gone, and maybe he would never come back! But that STILL left Maria on my team. She is the prettiest, most perfect girl in the whole school. Compared to her, I might as well be invisible. Whenever Maria was around, I felt skinnier, my teeth looked more bucked, and my hair seemed to turn into one gigantic frizz ball. I could never compare to her. And now we were on the same team. Maybe Rodney's outburst wasn't such a bad idea. Maybe I should have one of my own.

The only good thing that came out of that whole episode was that Miss Dollywog told our team that we could replace Rodney with a kid from another class, since most likely he was going to be suspended. Maybe even moved to another school. Ant, asked if Rodney could be moved to another state. We all laughed. Miss Dollywog, didn't answer, but we sure hoped that was the case.

One kid yelled, "I hope he goes to JAIL!"

"Yeah," we all chimed in.

Of course, Maria selected her brother Hector, who was in the fourth grade, and Ant wanted his friend Benjamin. Everybody liked Ant, so we agreed to let Benjamin join the team. But with a little push from me, the team also decided to let George and Joseph be on the team. George was in the fifth grade, but he really should have been in the sixth grade, but he got real sick in kindergarten and was held back 'cause he missed so many days. Joseph was in the fourth grade.

I'm glad Miss Dollywog said we could pick teammates from other classes. So now with my brothers on the team, I was sure that I would be elected team leader, and not Maria, who always got elected to everything!

We agreed to meet on Saturday at our house. Forgot to tell you, the Morrises let us have company (another first) and we could even play with our friends in the yard and pretend that the garage was our club house. A secret club house for our really special friends. We even had a secret handshake.

6

Aunt Hattie, Uncle Ed and Cousins Galore!

by Emma

Every Saturday the Morrises took us to visit Aunt Hattie and Uncle Ed. Joseph loved our new cousins — said they were "Neato!" And I guess I did too.

On every trip, George sang this crazy song that he made up:

"Got me some cousins,

Got me some friends,

Gonna use my magic,

So the day never ends."

I liked the song because it made Joseph and me laugh. George was a funny kid. Unfortunately, sometimes he'd add another verse to his song.

"Emma's so bossy. But she can't stop me from singing my song, 'cause we love the Morrises and calling them Mom and Dad ain't wrong!"

I smiled at him, but we both knew that he was going to pay for that.

Mrs. Morris always brought snacks for us to eat in the car. Like I said, that lady sure liked to feed us. And we sure liked to eat!

"Do you remember how to get there?" asked Mrs. Morris. But we all knew that Mr. Morris got lost ALL THE TIME.

"Of course, Mama, we go there all the time.

They had a really nice car, a blue and white Oldsmobile 98. It was the size of a school bus. We all like it 'cause it had really big seats in the back. No radio or heater, though, so on cold days we just snuggled up in the backseat under a blanket and munched on them snacks.

"Are you sure you remember how to get there?" asked Mrs. Morris again.

"Of course I remember. My memory isn't that bad!" he answered back. But instead of driving off, we just sat there. After a few minutes, Mr. Morris sighed and got out of the car and headed back to the house.

"What's the matter, aren't we going?" asked Joseph.

"He forgot the car keys," answered Mrs. Morris. "But don't tell him that I told you," she said smiling.

After a few minutes, we were on our way. But, of course we got lost! When we finally got to Aunt Hattie's house, our cousins "Squeegee, WallyBoy, BabyGirl, Sara Beth, Little James, GertieMae, and Harryre, ran into the big living room and started hugging us.

OMIGOSH! These people hug all the time, too! Good thing we liked them.

"Rewind" (that's their goofy looking Great Dane) followed them into the room. Then "Felix the cat" came from behind the sofa and started to rub against my legs. I tried to act like I liked that cat, but I really don't like animals. Not like George, who was nuts about dogs and all types of creatures.

I really hate dogs! I got my reasons. I'll tell you more about that later, but it has to do with one of them foster homes that had a REALLY big dog. Well it looked like a dog, but it didn't chase no sticks or play with balls or nothing. It was more like a big fat lump of hair with a tail.

Uncle Ed and Mr. Morris were brothers. They mostly talked about how not to get lost.

And Aunt Hattie? Boy, she was as good a cook as Mrs. Morris. She made the best fried chicken in the whole world. Back then they fried chicken with lard. Lard was a type of pig fat that folks used as a cooking fat or shortening, or even sometimes to spread on bread like butter. Yeah, it was pretty unhealthy, but we had "a lard of fun" eating that chicken. That's one of George's jokes.

We mostly played in the yard. Games like tag or sometimes freeze tag. Rewind chased us, begging for food. That's the dog, not one of our cousins, remember?

Boy, those afternoons sure went by fast. Luckily, Aunt Hattie always gave us a bag of fried chicken to take home and of course, a big hug. They were always nice to us. As we headed for the door, Aunt Hattie started talking to Mrs. Morris. "Gertie, you and Bill got you some real precious *cutie-pie-kids.*"

"Yeah! They're the best," said Mrs. Morris.

George and I looked at each other grinning from ear to ear, then ran down the stairs of the front porch to the car. Nobody had ever called us "the best." Are these people for real? I was always surprised at how much they liked us. So it seemed, anyway. ...

Mr. Morris was already in the car. He and Uncle Ed weren't much for long good byes.

"Hope you kids had fun," he said.

"Emma wants a dog," George yelled.

"Sure it's not YOU who wants a dog?" Mr. Morris asked.

"*Yup!* But Joseph wants one, too," George said looking me right in the eye. He had broken Rule #1: NEVER ASK FOR ANYTHING!!!

"Stop it!" I whispered in his ear.

But he ignored me, "You heard Aunt Hattie, we're cute and precious! Besides, it's only a dog. Don't you want a dog, sis?"

But instead of answering, I just looked out the window. I was losing control of my brothers. The Morrises had won their hearts!

We were headed for big trouble, I could feel it in my bones. I wish I could tell you that we didn't get lost on the way home, but by now you know that we did.

Despite my brother's outrageous behavior, it was still a really fun day. Tomorrow, I will set him straight, you can be sure of that!

7

I Hate Dogs
by Emma

I can't believe George. He's going to ruin it for all of us. I don't know what's worse, him breaking rule #1 (never ask for anything), or him not listening to me anymore. I am the oldest! What had gotten into my little brother? It was the first time George had deliberately ever broken a rule. And he was not even acting like he cared if I was mad. I felt a little scared. Okay, I felt REALLY SCARED!

And what about us? What is he thinking? He wants a dog?! Would the Morrises be able to care for a dog and US at the same time? Were they even going to keep us? I know what you're thinking, why doesn't she want a dog? Well, I guess for most kids they're fun. But for me, they're more bad memories with mean people.

Okay, so here it is: In one of our other foster homes, there was this dog named BoBo. He was some kind of pedigree (that's rich-folk talk for an expensive dog). That mangy mutt was treated like a HUMAN while we were treated more like DOGS! I forget the name of those foster people, probably on purpose, but I will NEVER forget the name of that dog. I used to call him "Booger" under my breath.

Can you believe they used to order the dog's food from the butcher shop? And lucky me, I was in charge of cooking it. BoBo was eating special food, while we were eating hot dogs that blew up to the size of baseball bats when you cooked them. Those franks tasted like they were made out of sawdust, so I doubt if they were even made from meat! So when nobody was looking, I ate as much of BoBo's food as I could. He would stare up at me as if he knew, but lucky for me, he couldn't talk, and I sure as snot never told a soul. Not even my brothers. To this day, not only do I hate real dogs, but I also hate hot dogs. So as long as I'm in charge of my brothers there will be no dogs!

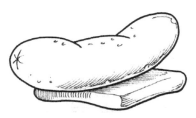

8

We Get a Dog!
(What's Wrong With This Picture?)
by Emma

Just two weeks later, my worst fear happened.

"Get up you sleepy heads," laughed Mrs. Morris. "Today, we are going to get us a dog!!"

George leaped out of bed, ran to my room, and screamed, "I told you Emma, my magic powers are working again!" I was stunned. No Way! This must be a trick. But the boys got dressed and ate their breakfast in record time. I was too upset to be hungry.

As usual, Mr. Morris was already in the car.

"Bill, do you know where you're going?" asked Mrs. Morris,

"Of course, Mama." That's what he always said.

"Do you have your car keys?" asked Joseph.

Silence. Mr. Morris burst out laughing. We all started to laugh too. In one of those other foster homes, we'd probably be getting a spanking for even making a joke about grown folks.

Anyway, yes he DID have his keys, but like always, he got lost. Especially when he was driving to new places. Sometimes he even got lost on walks. Mr. Morris told us that he had trouble following directions, especially maps. Said that some of the wires in his brain must have gotten mixed up when he got hit in the head by a ball as a kid. *Yup!* Mixed up!

So as usual, it took us forever to get to the animal shelter. And it seemed even longer because, since George had broken the rule, I refused to speak. I thought that would scare him into silence. But it got worse!

He had the nerve to act like *HE* was in charge. He got out of the car and walked into the shelter like he owned the place. The shelter was a big old warehouse in another part of town.

"It smells stinky," said Joseph.

Well, what did he expect? Flowers? There were lots and lots of cats and dogs in cages. Big ones, little ones, kittens, puppies. ... We walked around to see if we could find just the right dog to take home. Something cute and fun. Mrs. Morris said we needed a dog that was well-trained.

Mr. Morris said, "we should pick with our hearts."

What the heck does that mean? If I picked with my heart, we wouldn't be getting no dumb dog in the first place!

Then in the back of the room, we saw a sign that said: "Special Friends: Get a $5 Bonus If you adopt one of us!"

"Gertie, kids, let's go over there," Mr. Morris said pointing to the sign.

We looked inside one of the cages and all we could see was a blur. Something was moving, and FAST! Flipping, jumping and rolling over like it had fleas up the *wazoo!* Then it stopped. Inside the cage was the cutest brown dog I've ever seen. His two front paws were white and it looked like he was wearing boxing gloves. When the attendant saw us looking, he came over and told us everything he knew about the dog.

"He's a pedigree Boxer — been here for months! His name is Sidney and they tell me he's REAL smart. The people who left him here used to travel with the Circus. But his owner got sick, so the family brought him to us. But we can't seem to find him a home. Folks keep bringing him back. He's kind of difficult to handle, they say."

"Just like us!" blurted out Joseph.

"Can we have him? Pleeeease?" George begged. "He's so beautiful, and he needs a home."

I just stood there. This dog is trouble, I thought — even if he IS cute.

"We'll take him." said Mr. Morris. I looked at Mrs. Morris, for sure she would say no. That dog looked anything but trained. But she smiled and nodded yes.

"Are you sure?" the attendant asked?

"Are you REALLY sure?" I asked.

Mr. Morris didn't even hesitate. "My kids want that dog, so that's the dog we're getting."

George was so happy he started yelling, "This is even better than when I made that rabbit disappear! My magic powers are back!"

I was speechless.

A dog named Sidney now had the power to make us lose the only hope we ever had of being kept. That's why I'm so careful and I always watch and wait. Because bad stuff always happens, and the next thing you know you got no place to live!

George and Joseph tried to hug me, but I wasn't having it! I continued to give them the silent death ray treatment.

Then George whispered in my ear. "If you don't have the things you want, at least be grateful for all the things you don't have and you don't want."

What in the *cockamamie* does that mean? Like if I'm not happy that we're getting a dog, then at least I should be happy that I don't have chicken pox or something? Why won't he just speak English?

See what I mean? That dumb *ol'* dog is already making him crazy!

9

Team Meeting: War
by Emma

Getting that stupid dog really made it hard for George and Joseph to focus on the Sixth Grade Project. Mr. Morris said we could have our team meetings in the garage, so we had our first meeting on a Saturday afternoon after we got home from seeing Aunt Hattie and Uncle Ed. Everyone showed up on time, which was great. Mrs. Morris made us cookies, which was even better. Maybe it would be okay, maybe my dog-loving brothers would calm down and focus on the project. First we had to think of a name for our team.

"Well," said George, "it's called the Dream Gift Project, so why not call ourselves the "Dream Team?" Everyone loved George's idea. Hey, that's not bad.

I chimed in, "Okay, but we need a slogan to put under our name — something that we can put on posters and nail on fences in the neighborhood. Again, George was quick as lightning and suggested "It will take Teamwork to Make the Dream Work!"

Wow! He's really good at this! I can't believe these great ideas are coming from MY younger brother. The same kid who thinks he made a rabbit disappear. He should do this for a living when he grows up! There must be a job where you can just think of great sayings that people would pay lots of money for.

The next thing we needed to decide was who would be the team leader? Well, I knew it SHOULD be me. And I already knew it WOULD be me because I'll get the most votes. I know that George, Joseph and, for sure, Ant would vote for me. At least I thought so until George opened up his mouth again. But this time what came out WASN'T so great.

"I nominate Maria!" he said.

SHOCKAROONEY!!!

Do you believe that? My own brother — a traitor!!! It was just as I suspected all along. George was gaga about Maria just like all the other boys in school. How could I ever compete with that?! Just wait till everyone leaves! There was no Rule #3, but I was sure as heck *gonna* make one. "Never vote for anyone but your brother or sister!"

First meeting - first PROBLEM! The battle was now officially *ON!*

"Well I nominate Emma," said Ant.

That's better. "I should be team leader," I said with great confidence, "because I won the Good Citizen essay contest."

Maria stood up and said, "That's nice, Emma, but we all know that since I'M class president AND I won the spelling bee AND the fire safety contest, *I* should be team leader!"

Now I was desperate! "Well I'll be thirteen in March, and that makes me the oldest!" I yelled! Good move I thought, who could argue with that? It's a fact! Everyone knows that the oldest kid should be in charge!

Then Maria smirked and shouted, "Thirteen and you're STILL in the sixth grade? Then you must have been LEFT BACK! Yes, that makes you a great choice, Emma. I'm sure our group will be in great hands."

Oh NO! How did she know?!! My stomach twisted into a knot. My forehead got covered in a layer of cold sweat. I felt ill.

Suddenly the roof of the garage flew off and a giant fire-breathing dragon swooped down and swallowed Maria up.

CHOMP!!

She was gone. For good! My problem was solved.

Well ... not really ... but I can wish, can't I?

I didn't know what to say, so I ran out of the garage and hid under my bed for the next two years. Okay, so maybe it was only until dinner, but the point is that I got away from *little Miss Perfect* and my brother the traitor. They deserve each other.

Maria was right. I did get left back. But it's not because I'm not smart. I got nothing but A's and B's on my report card this year. Same for most every year. But it was that stupid dog's fault. You know, the one I told you about — *Booger.*

Not only didn't they feed us, but I spent so much time having to do work around the house, and taking care of that beast, that I NEVER had time to study. I tried to tell my foster parents that I really wanted to do well in school, but do you know what they told me? They said that "girls didn't need to learn to do anything but how to cook and clean." That way when I got married, I'd already know how to be a good wife. Do you believe that?!

It was all their fault! That was one of the worst homes ever. Plus we moved around a lot that year, and every time we did, we had to get used to a whole new school. That's not easy.

Thank goodness that George had also been held back, or we would be in the same grade. I know that sounds really selfish to wish that something bad should happen to someone else just because it happens to you, but it would be really embarrassing to be in the same class with my younger brother. He'd never let me live that down.

See what I mean?

Trouble already.

That's why *I hate dogs!*

10

Who Knew?
by Emma

No team meetings for me, ever again — I *ain't* never going to those meetings again!

After we came back from Aunt Hattie's on Saturday, I went straight to my room. Then I heard Mrs. Morris call for me to come downstairs. "Emma, your friends are here."

"I don't have any friends, and I'm not coming down!" I said pouting.

"Yes you are, young lady, come down here. NOW!"

Uh-oh. Mrs. Morris never spoke mean like that. ... Never! But my mind was made up! I didn't move, until I heard her coming up the stairs. By the time Mrs. Morris opened the door to my room, I was hiding under the bed. She figured it out pretty quickly, and laid down on the floor right next to the bed. Our eyes were staring at each other.

"Emma," she said, "I know you are upset about what happened with the team last week, your brother Joseph told me."

"So, what do you care? What does anybody care?! Besides, you're not my real mother anyway!" The words just seemed to pop out of my mouth all by themselves. I couldn't help it.

Mrs. Morris gasped as the words reached her ears, and she sat up and put her hand to her cheek. There was a long silence, like she was trying to think of what to say. Was she going to yell? Was she going to cry? At that moment I wished I could have just curled up in a ball and disappeared.

Finally, she spoke. "But I WANT to be, Emma. I am not trying to replace your real mother, but I just want to love you like a mother. There is a difference."

Then the worse thing happened. Mrs. Morris DID start to cry. Tears were rolling down her round cheeks and onto her neck. Mrs. Morris would always said, "the soul produces a rainbow, when the eyes produce tears." (It wasn't until I was all grown up that I really understood what that saying meant. A good cry is like rain, it just rinses away the pain, then a rainbow appears. And at the end of the rainbow there's a pot of gold! At least I think that's what that means. Boy, my family sure has a lot of sayings.)

I started to cry, too. Big hot tears that rolled out of my eyes, down my cheeks and onto the floor. I can't believe I said that. I felt really awful. She had been good to us — so good — and I was being mean. Mean like the people who had been mean to us in those homes. People who didn't want us and sent us back. Mean like some of the bad kids at school who called us names.

I crawled out from under my bed and hugged her so tight. I was happy when she hugged me back. Then she handed me some tissues to wipe my tears. She wiped hers, too. After a few minutes, we went downstairs. Together. Maria and Hector were in the living room. Some friends! I thought.

"Tell her, Maria." said Hector.

Maria said nothing.

"Tell her, or I will," he said.

Maria spoke in a whisper. "I knew what happened to you, because I'll be thirteen in February.

OMIGOSH! MARIA had been LEFT BACK too! I didn't know what to say, so we just stood there in silence.

"How come you never liked me?" asked Maria.

"I don't know," I said while looking down at my feet. But I DID know. I didn't like Maria because she had everything. Not only was she the prettiest girl in the school, but she had a REAL family. How lucky can one kid be? It just wasn't fair.

Hector put his hand on my shoulder. "We're sorry, Emma. Please come back to the team. Everybody misses you, and we need you."

"Really?" I asked.

"Yes. Really!" Maria said.

What could I do? My team needed me! Mrs. Morris gave us some ice cream and the three of us went out to the garage to join the others. Anyway, being alone is no fun. It's kind of icky once you get used to having friends. When I walked into the garage, everyone cheered.

"Hey, Emma's back!" said Ant. I felt better already. We quickly got down to business. Hector was in charge of the nominations.

Ant started it off. He raised his hand and said, "I nominate myself to be in charge of something!"

"What in the *cockamamie* is SOMETHING?????" asked Hector.

Ant replied. "I *dunno*, I just want to be in charge of something. Something BIG! Like my brains!"

"You mean like your big head," laughed Hector.

"Hey, that's mean!" Cathy-Jane yelled. After that, all I heard was arguing.

"No it isn't. ... Yes it is. ... Your head IS big. ... Yeah well your MOUTH is bigger. ... *blah blah blah.* ..." It was a mess! We were doomed!

Then Sam Lee jumped up, stormed to the front of the garage and pounded his fist against the lid of the garbage can. He had a brown belt in Karate, so nobody said a word.

"STOP IT!" he said.

Sidney followed him barking and jumping. He must have thought that Sam Lee wanted to play. But one look from Sam Lee, and Sidney knew that wasn't the case. He sat down and lowered his head. Everyone gasped because Sam Lee was usually very quiet. And, Sidney, well, he never listened to anyone, except when he wanted a treat. That dog would do anything for a treat.

"Teams are supposed to work together," Sam Lee said. "But, if you guys want to keep fighting, then why don't we call ourselves *The Mean Team* and just forget about the kids in the hospital?!"

He was right. We were all so glad when Rodney left the team because we thought he would be a terror.

"Yeah, look at us. We're no better than Rodney," I said sadly.

"*Nope*, but at least we smell better," said Ant. That made everyone laugh. We really needed that.

"We are NOT a *mean team*. We are the *DREAM TEAM!!!*" said Maria once the laughter stopped. "And those kids are going to get the best toys ever, cause we are going to raise enough money to buy every kid in that hospital a toy!"

We decided to have our elections, and believe it or not, everything worked out fine. Take a look:

Team Officers

Team Leaders: Maria and Emma. (Sometimes you *gotta* just do what you *gotta* do.)

Director of Finances: ANT

Project Ideas: The whole team!

Later on, after we decided on our project, we could just pick what we wanted to do — no fights. Of course, I would still be the leader ... well ... Maria and I. We were finally a team. Now all we needed was a great idea so we *thunk* as hard as we could!

And our ideas were plenty good:

"Lemonade stand."

"Boring," shouted Hector.

"Bake sale."

"No way! Bet a billion teams are going to do that," yelled Benjamin.

"Besides, have you ever tasted C J 's cookies?!" asked Maria.

"Hey!" said Cathy-Jane.

"Talent show," yelled George!

"What talent?" asked Cathy-Jane.

"Sidney!" answered Sam Lee. "We've got Sidney! I bet we could teach him to do tricks."

"Sure, he WAS in the circus," said George. He might even know some tricks already."

"The man at the shelter said he traveled WITH the circus, that's not the same thing," I said.

"Is too!" said Joseph taking his two fingers out of his mouth.

"Well, let's see!" George ran up to the front of the garage, and threw a ball in the air. Sidney stood up on his hind legs, twirled around and jumped straight into the air while catching it in his mouth! We couldn't believe our eyes!

"See? I TOLD you!" George said smiling. "Sidney is a magic dog, I knew it the first time I saw him!"

Then Joseph jumped on top of a crate and started waving his arms. "I can teach him Superhero stuff."

"And I could also make him disappear!" said George. "But I don't want him to be gone forever like Bubba."

"Who's Bubba?" they asked.

"Long story," I said. "I'll tell you later." But I was hoping they'd forget to ask.

"I could teach him Karate and maybe even how to box," said Sam Lee.

"That's it!" yelled Ant. "We're *gonna* have us a circus! The Greatest Circus on Earth featuring *Sidney the Boxing Boxer*!"

It was a slam dunk of an idea! Elections for the next jobs were easy as pie:

Directors of Talent: Sam Lee, George and Joseph

Set Designers: C J & Benjamin

Advertising: Emma and George

Costumes: Maria

We handed in our plans to Miss Dollywog, five whole days before the deadline.

11

Top Secret
by Emma

Sam Lee, George and Joseph met everyday after school to train Sidney. They wouldn't let us watch. Said it was "TOP SECRET."

But after two weeks of training, Sidney started hiding in the basement. Some mornings when George went to walk him, Sidney wasn't even in the yard — his favorite place to sleep when the weather was nice.

One day we searched the neighborhood, but he was nowhere to be found. Eventually he returned wagging his tail and ready to begin practicing his tricks. After we gave him treats, of course.

Boy, that dog would do anything for TREATS!

Unfortunately, it wasn't just the boys who were so secretive. Maria wouldn't let us see the costumes she was designing either!

"TOP SECRET," she said.

Great! Another surprise! Sometimes Maria is a show off! But I must admit she did have style. Plus she had the prettiest clothes in the whole school, the longest hair, and she even had … you know … boobs. That girl really got under my skin.

Hector, Cathy-Jane and Mr. Morris started building a boxing ring out of ropes and a few fence posts. Mr. Morris even built a stage out of wood for the boxing scene. It was portable, so it would be easy to take to school and set up.

Me? I made sure everything got done. I was in charge of everything. It just sort of happened that way. Just the way it had always been. I am *sooo* terrific at being in charge!

We decided it was time put up posters. So Maria and I sat down to design a flyer. After all, the more people who came to our circus, the more money we would raise.

Although Maria and I were still a little stiff with each other, the one thing that we *both* wanted was to win!

12

A Close Call

by Emma

"Emma, George, and Joseph, come downstairs!" It was Mrs. Morris. She sounded UPSET! When we got to the kitchen, it was a mess!

"Sugar foot and candy canes!!!" yelled Mrs. Morris. She always said that when she was upset. "What are we to do with this dog?" she asked. Mrs. Morris seemed really mad! Sidney had pulled everything out of the cabinets looking for treats. Flour, sugar, beans and cereal were everywhere! Now he was hiding under the table with syrup dripping from his mouth and flour all over his nose. He looked scared. I think we ALL were!

"You're taking him back to the animal shelter aren't you?" cried Joseph.

George screamed, "NO! You can't. He didn't mean it!"

Mrs. Morris looked at the boys, then looked at me.

"Emma, what should we do about this?"

She was asking ME?

"Ummm ... well ... maybe he shouldn't get treats for a week!!" I replied. I didn't really think she'd get rid of Sidney. For some reason, I wasn't worried anymore about a lot of the things that I used to worry about all the time. I never told my brothers what happened between me and Mrs. Morris. You know, the time I made her cry? Then she said all those really nice things about being a mother, and love and stuff. I guess I just didn't want to get their hopes up. That way if we did get sent back to the shelter, I would be the only one whose hopes would be crushed. At least that was my plan. But after that, I felt a lot more relaxed about staying here forever. My brothers would see, everything was going to be fine! I just knew it.

Joseph was under the table holding Sidney and crying. Meanwhile George was trying not to cry, but tears were streaming down his face, too. Mrs. Morris told us all to go out onto the porch. Sidney crawled from under the table, with his tail between his legs and followed us.

She grabbed us real close and kissed us, and said, "We don't send back family — EVER! Family is forever and trouble don't change that! Sidney has been a bad boy, but he's just a dog so we got to love him and make sure he knows not to get into my stuff ... or I will fry him in butter and serve him for lunch!"

Silence.

Finally she smiled.

WHEW! Then we all got it! Mrs. Morris was joking. She would never even hurt a flea.

"Now you children go clean up that dog and this mess."

See, I was right, Mrs. Morris IS a great mom. ... *Uhh,* did I say "Mom"?

OMIGOSH! Rule #2, broken by yours truly!

Who would have thunk it!

13

The Greatest Show on Earth: Act One

by Emma

The day of the show had finally come! We all agreed to meet at the school around noon so we could rehearse our show one last time. Plus Maria and Benjamin were FINALLY going to let us see the costumes.

By one o'clock, all the teams were running around like crazy trying to set up before they let the crowd into the schoolyard. We could see stands for lemonade, pie-eating contests, juggling, and tons of stuff for sale; everything from balloons to brownies. It was kind of hard to focus with all the great smells in the air. Especially freshly-popped popcorn (one of the best smells on earth). And cotton candy, too! But the grandest booth was the ice-cream booth. It was huge, with cone-shaped statues and posters with drawings of all types of ice-cream goodies. Impressive! Even if they were our competition.

Our posters had worked and kids were lined up to buy tickets. And boy did they! We sold out immediately! And there were still a ton of kids standing outside the gate waiting to get in. Mrs. Morris had asked the school if we could use some of the folding chairs from the auditorium, so the people could sit down. Since we were the only team putting on a full-fledged show, they agreed and the people piled in like ants. Oops, no disrespect to our friend Ant.

By the way, Ant came up with a brilliant idea. He charged anyone who wanted to see our show, but who couldn't get a seat, only 15 cents. He said it was the standing-room price. I told you, Ant is a wizard when it comes to math!

In the very first row, right in the middle, sat Mr. and Mrs. Morris, Aunt Hattie, Uncle Ed and all our cousins. They waved but I was too nervous to wave back. It made me feel good to see them though. To see OUR family. Imagine that. Finally, it was Show Time!!!

Hector was the Master of Ceremonies and looked real cool in his top hat and white jacket. You should have seen him!

"Ladies and Gentlemen, and children of all ages," he shouted.

"I present 'Sidney — The Incredible Circus Dog of the Century!'"

George led Sidney into the ring. He was wearing a collar with red balls hanging off it, and blue cuffs on his paws. George had on his black hat, a black jacket, a red shirt and white pants. They both looked just like circus performers. And I had on my pretty red dress, you know, the one I told you I got for Christmas?

"Go, Sidney!" Hector yelled as he threw the Frisbee in the air!

But SIDNEY just laid down and put his head between his paws while the Frisbee sailed over his head. Oh NO! My heart sunk into my sneakers. The rest of the team looked like they were going to faint!

"Roll over!" shouted Hector. NOTHING! ... Sidney didn't move a hair. In fact he started whimpering. I don't know about the rest of my team, but I started to get a cold feeling over my body. And my hands started to sweat. I KNEW I shouldn't have believed in no dumb dog. I keep telling you, they're bad luck! Sidney got up and turned his back to the audience! But he never did that in rehearsal. Ever!

Do dogs get nervous? I know they go to heaven, but do they get afraid, like us?

Everyone on the team turned green as the audience started to laugh. Then they started to boo! Then something happened. Outside the gate, I saw RODNEY laughing his head off!

"Hey, Vanilla, maybe your star needs something to get him started!" he yelled at the top of his lungs!

Everyone heard it. I could have died. Then he took something out of his pocket. It was a whistle. I know because he blew it as loud as he could. Everyone in the audience covered their ears. Now he was laughing so hard he fell on the ground.

Suddenly, Sidney jumped to his feet, grabbed the Frisbee, tossed it into the air himself, then jumped in the air and caught it. The crowd *"ooohed."* We all looked at each other, then we looked at Sidney. We didn't even know he could do that!

"Drum roll please," said Hector.

Benjamin beat on the garbage cans and the audience started stomping their feet. The louder the drum beat, the more Sidney performed. And if you thought that WE were surprised, you should have seen Rodney! I guess that performing in front of all of these people made Sidney think that he was back in the circus.

And maybe that's how they got him to do tricks, with a whistle and a drum roll! Who knows? But what we DID know was that even though he was trying to be mean, Rodney had saved the show! I looked over at him. Then I saw Mrs. Morris get up and walk towards the gate.

When Rodney saw her, he froze like a statue. Mrs. Morris whispered something to Rodney through the gate, he handed her the whistle and ran off like the police were chasing him.

"Ant, go get the whistle from my mom," I said while pointing at Mrs. Morris. "It looks like we're going to need it."

Ant ran over, got the whistle and brought it back.

Next Joseph ran onto the stage dressed in his new Superman costume.

"Go, Sidney!" he shouted.

I nudged Ant with my elbow and told him to blow the whistle. None of us were sure if we had to blow it every single time, but we didn't want to take any chances. So that's what he did. After he wiped it off first. Guess he didn't want to get any of Rodney's germs. I can't say I blame him.

Sidney twirled on his two hind legs. He even did flips and jumped through the hula hoops that we had lined up. Okay, now we were REALLY surprised 'cause he never even did that in rehearsal either. At least that's what George told me during intermission.

Then CJ ran onto the stage screaming. (Don't worry, it's all part of the show.) She was pretending to be chased by an evil monster. But it was really just Benjamin in a scary mask and wearing swim fins. His favorite movie was a horror film called, "Creature from the Black Lagoon," so that's what he was trying to be.

I nudged Ant again, and as soon as he blew the whistle, Sidney climbed on top of a crate — his superhero cape (that Maria put on him) was flying in the wind that was coming from a fan that we had set up — then he jumped and knocked the monster to the ground! CJ was saved!

The crowd roared! In fact, they yelled so loud that even kids from some of the other booths came over to watch our show. I think the whole place must have shut down to watch us.

The coolest part of it all was this was all of our ideas coming together. It really was like a dream come true. George was right, it really does "take teamwork to make the dream work!"

When Sidney finally sat up and clapped his front paws, we had to stop the kids from running onto the stage to pet him. Hector announced to the crowd that it was intermission and that we needed to set up for the second half of The Greatest Circus on Earth!

Intermission

We all huddled around Sidney and hugged him. We couldn't believe what we just saw. We could still hear the crowd chanting his name, "Sid-ney, Sid-ney, Sid-ney."

This was *wayyyy* better than any of us could have ever imagined. I looked out into the audience. Mrs. Morris was back in her seat. She blew me a kiss and Mr. Morris gave me a thumbs up sign. This time I waved back at them and also to our cousins who were still clapping and stomping their feet.

Joseph filled up Sidney's water dish so he would be fresh for the second half. *Shucks*, after what we just witnessed, I think we ALL could have used a drink of water!

Emma

Act II

After the intermission, it was George's turn to perform his big magic trick. He looked so keen with his black hat, and cape. Mrs. Morris had made sure they were nice and clean. They almost looked like new. He started with a bunch of his favorite card tricks. The crowd liked it, but what they really wanted to see was Sidney. When George was done, they got their wish.

Joseph led Sidney back in the ring. The crowd went crazy! I think that George thought it was for him because he took another bow. My brother is SUCH a ham! You've got to admire a kid with that much style.

I nudged Ant again, and he blew the whistle. Sidney climbed into a huge cardboard box that Cathy-Jane and Benjamin had decorated. George waved his magic wand. Ant blew the whistle again — then moved the box.

POOF! Sidney had disappeared! Well not really! But he wasn't in the box anymore. He had crawled out through a flap in the back of the box. Then Joseph gave his leash a tug to get him to hide under the table with him. We had covered the table with one of Mrs. Morris' old table cloths, so nobody saw them. But don't tell anyone I told you. The crowd went nuts!

Hector walked to the center of the ring and announced, "Now for the Grand Finale! For the first time anywhere, The Dream Team presents the **Match of the Century** between the reigning champ Sam Lee: The Karate King and the challenger — Fearless Sidney: The Boxing Boxer."

The response from the audience was awesome! Kids were screaming with excitement! Even some of the parents in the audience were cheering as both fighters entered the ring and ran to their corners. Sidney was wearing white and red satin shorts and a green robe.

I don't know HOW Maria got Sidney to let her put them shorts and robe on him, but he looked cool in his outfit! He sat on a stool, and Joseph put tiny boxing gloves on his front two paws! Well, they were really socks that Mrs. Morris had made to look like professional boxing gloves.

Sam Lee was wearing black shorts, and he had on real boxing gloves that his dad used to use when he was a boxer! He took a bow, removed his robe and Championship Belt that Maria made for him. Ant gave him a drink of water then tied on his boxing gloves, Sam Lee waved to the yelling crowd. George hit the old cow bell that we had borrowed from Uncle Ed. The fight was on! The fighters ran toward each other. Sidney was upright on his hind legs — his front paws swinging. He'd land on all fours then hop back up and walk on two legs again as long as he could. Hector gave a blow-by-blow description of the fight.

"Folks, the fighters are jabbing and weaving. Sidney has to be careful not to let Sam Lee land his famous karate chop punch to his snout. Too late! Sam Lee: The Karate King lands a blow to Sidney's jaw!" (Don't worry, it was only a pretend hit, Sam Lee would never hurt Sidney!)

"Down goes the challenger!" yelled Hector.

Sidney laid on his back like he was dead. All his paws were up in the air! It was hilarious!

"Ladies and gentlemen, this fight might be over!!!!" yelled Hector.

You should have seen Sidney, that dog is a born actor. Who knew?! The crowd started to shout! "Get up, Sidney!" He didn't move!

Ant blew the whistle again. Suddenly Sidney's ears perked up and then he got up.

Hector continued, "Folks, he's up! Sam Lee is heading towards him.

I can't believe my eyes! Sidney is charging. He just landed a blow to the champ's chest! Sam Lee: The Karate King is stumbling; Sidney is finishing him off with right paw to the jaw. The Champ is down!" Hector, started the count:

"One ... two ... three ..."

Sam Lee pretended like he was trying to get up. You know, he can act pretty good himself. Not as good as Sidney, but not bad either. The count continued, "Four ... five ... six ..."

Sam Lee moaned, but he stayed down. Now the crowd joined in the count, "Seven ... eight ... nine ... TEN!" Sam Lee let his head roll to the side like he was knocked out!

Hector grabbed Sidney's front paw and announced:

"The winner BY A KNOCKOUT, and the NEW heavyweight champion of the world ... Sidney the Boxing Boxer!"

The crowd was up and shouting: *"SIDNEY, SIDNEY!"*

OMIGOSH! I have to admit, our show was incredible! And the audience must have thought so too, because all the kids were rushing into the ring. It couldn't have been better if we dreamed it! I looked around and everyone was cheering. And to my surprise, in the back of the yard, was Rodney. He had snuck back in to see the show. And he was clapping, too! But as soon as he realized, I was looking at him, he stopped and started to walk away. I wanted to call out to him, but the noise of the crowd was too loud. It was at that moment that I realized how badly Rodney wanted to belong. I guess he just wanted the same thing all kids wanted, friends and people who saw the good in him.

After I hugged Sidney and Sam Lee, the first person I looked for was Mrs. Morris. Not only did she protect us from Rodney, but she also got the whistle for us. She and Mr. Morris came over to the three of us and ... you guessed it, they gave us a big hug. And we all hugged them back as tight as we could. This was one of the happiest moments of our entire lives! Me and my brothers just grinned at one another.

You know, the kind of grin that says, *ain't we grand?!*

14

The Awards Assembly

by Emma

On Monday, the whole school was still talking about OUR show. I don't know about George and Joseph, but I don't think I slept a wink that entire weekend. We couldn't wait for the Awards Assembly. And even though the winning team would not be announced yet, the whole school was buzzing about who they thought would win the Sixth Grade Project. Kids came up to us and said how much they liked our show. Everybody said we were sure to be the winners.

When the day finally arrived, we were still all really nervous. It was weird because we never had that feeling for something good before. Usually if we're nervous, it's because we knew something bad was going to happen. After the morning announcements, the whole school piled into the auditorium.

Principal Johnson walked up on the stage. "All right, children, I know you're all very excited." She waited a few more minutes until the auditorium was so quiet you could hear fleas fly.

Principal Johnson congratulated everyone on what a great job we all had done with our projects. I *sorta* blanked out after that so I'm not sure exactly WHAT she said. Probably talked about how much money we raised and how happy the kids at the hospital would be with their gifts. I wanted to listen, I really did, but all I could think about was the award! The only team that I was really worried about was the group that served homemade ice cream and it had been rumored that they had made a bundle of money, too.

They called themselves, "The Cream Team." Do you believe that? What a rip off.

Finally, the moment we had all been waiting for: "the winning team is from Miss Dollywog's class, so I'd like her to come up and present the award to her students."

Yes! That means it's definitely not the Cream Team! It seemed like an eternity for Miss Dollywog to get to the stage, it was killing us!!!

Then she started talking, *"blah blah blah ..."* After a couple of minutes we finally heard the sentence that every kid in the auditorium was dying to hear "And the winning team is ..."

It seemed like she paused for a million years. The suspense was killing us!

"The Dream Team, who raised $63.50!" she said. Finally!

We did it. We won!!!

"Maria Gonzales, Emma, George and Joseph Fraser, Anthony Smith, Cathy-Jane Johnson, Benjamin Smalls, Hector Gonzalez, Sam Lee Chin, please come up."

We ran down the aisle and onto the stage. Miss Dollywog told us that the team leader should say a few words.

Maria looked at me and said, "Emma you should be the one to talk." I was shocked! And to think, I used to think she was ... well, you know what I used to think. But that's water under the bridge as Mrs. Morris always says. That means instead of looking backwards, you should look forward. I think.

I took the microphone. My hands were shaking. "I'd like to thank you all for coming out to support us. Without you we couldn't have won. And I'd also like to thank all of my teammates, you guys were amazing! Plus I want to thank my dog Sidney, the best dog in the whole wide world."

The kids started chanting, *"Sid-ney, Sid-ney, Sid-ney!"*

And while the audience was applauding Sidney. I looked to the back of the auditorium and saw someone sitting in the very last row all by himself. It was Rodney. No one had seen him since the circus. For some reason he reminded me of when we first got Sidney, how he was all alone and nobody but us wanted him. I knew exactly what to do.

"There's one more very important person who we need to thank. I want to bring up one of our original teammates — the person who saved our show ... Rodney Callahan. Come on up and take a bow with your team."

The crowd went silent.

"It was Rodney who showed us how to train Sidney by using

his whistle. He even let us keep it. Let's all give him a really big hand." I started clapping. Then everyone else did too. Slowly at first, then like they meant it.

Rodney stood up, rubbing the back of his head. Then he started walking down the aisle towards the stage. Everyone was still clapping. When he got close to the stage, he did something I had never seen him do before. He smiled. And you know what, he was actually kinda cute! He came up onto the stage and me and the rest of the Dream Team gave him a nice big hug. *Jeepers!* The Morrises must really be rubbing off on us. Now we hug as much as they do.

But from the way that Rodney tensed up like a board, you'd think this was the first hug that he had ever gotten in his whole life! And you know what? Maybe it was. We don't know anything about him. Just like our friends don't know all the awful stuff that's happened to me and my brothers.

"Do you want to say something?" I asked him.

He smiled and shook his head no, then looked down at the floor. I'd never seen him act like that before.

"Thanks Emma," he said softly.

Did he just call me Emma? You mean he knows my name is not really Vanilla? Wow!

After the assembly, I asked Rodney where he had been? He said that he was in a school for kids who needed special help, but that if he was good, we might just see him in next year. I felt my heart thump. I was actually looking forward to seeing him in school next year. Especially since now, not only was he ACTING like a human being, but now he even SMELLED like one! No more rotten eggs. His clothes were clean, and he had combed his hair. Rodney was really handsome. Then I saw that Maria was smiling at him. What's that about?

Next, it was picture-taking time. And the whole group was included, even Rodney. Principal Johnson and Miss Dollywog congratulated us again and thanked all the teams for their hard work. We all bowed and went back to our seats.

If I didn't know better, I'd think I saw Rodney wipe a tear from the corner of his eye. This must be how the Morrises feel when they do stuff to make us happy. No wonder they like it. It feels really good.

I know what you're saying, it's just a dumb ol' school project, how can they be THAT happy? Mr. Morris always says, "Never judge anyone until you walk a mile in their shoes."

That means that you shouldn't think you know everything about someone until you really know how they live. So when you think about all the things me and my brothers have shared with you, it would have been easy for us to give up. It would have been easy for us not to do good in school, or to get in trouble, or give up, or lose hope. But that's not how it happened. In life, some things you have control over, and some things you don't. Just do the best you can.

But even though this was only a school project, it was the only thing that we had ever won in our lives. And it was the first time that we ever got so much attention and so much love. Being with the Morrises changed our lives.

The next day, Principal Johnson invited our team to her office. To our surprise, she told us that she had received so many calls requesting that we give another show that she wanted us to do it again. The principal said, that there was also a possibility that the local television station and newspapers would be at the show, and maybe we would be on television.

YIPES! TELEVISION! Our team was going to be on TV! Now we were going to be REALLY famous ... stars ... celebrities!

When the news got out, some of the other teams asked if they could set up their stands and sell stuff at our show.

Joseph protested! "No! Especially not The Cream Team? NO WAY!" he cried! After all, why should we help them?

But George reminded us that it took, "Teamwork to Make the Dream Work."

Sam Lee agreed. "Yeah, then we could all be winners, especially the kids in the hospital if we work together."

You know, not only had this experience made me look at Rodney differently ... and Maria, but this whole thing also made me look at George differently. He really did have a good head on his shoulders. Like I said before, George was a cheery kid, and he had a big heart. So we said yes and told the principal that the other teams could sell their stuff at our second show.

After the Awards Assembly, Rodney started hanging around with us after school. Not all the time, but enough. Rodney had changed, and Mrs. Morris said that he was glowing. Yeah, now I know what glowing means. Sam Lee said it was because Rodney finally took a bath. But I know there was more to it than that, because he told me that it was nice to have friends and to be invited to other kids' houses.

I think it was at that moment that I realized one of the most important lessons of my life: Everybody really wants the same thing — to be accepted, and to be loved.

15

The Show Must Go On Again
by Emma

Today is the day of our command performance! Mr. Morris wanted to meet Uncle Ed at the crack of dawn to set up our ring in the schoolyard again. None of us knew why they wanted to do it so early, but he said he had to run an errand afterwards and wanted to be back in time for the show.

But Sidney was nowhere to be found.

PANIC!!!!

Mr. Morris said he would find him before he went on his errand.

"You?! Of all people want to find someone's who's lost?!" moaned Mrs. Morris rubbing her forehead in disbelief. "Aren't you the King of Getting Lost, my dear?!"

"Exactly," replied Mr. Morris. "Who better to find someone who's lost than someone who gets lost all the time?"

Made sense to me. Mr. Morris got into the Oldsmobile to start the search. But instead of starting the car, he just sat there. After a minute or so, he got out and headed back towards the house. When he got to the top of porch, Mrs. Morris handed him his car keys. He smiled, got back in the car, and drove off.

An hour later, Mr. Morris came back with Sidney, PLUS he had another dog! A cute white Poodle. What was that about? But we were running late, so we just patted her on the head and continued packing our things for the big show. Mr. Morris dropped off both dogs then got back in the car and headed off on his errand. He said he had arranged for Uncle Ed to pick us up in case he wasn't back in time.

So Uncle Ed came to pick us up at noon. We decided to leave the Poodle in the yard. But not before Mrs. Morris gave her a bowl of water and a some food. Boy, it doesn't matter if you're a person or a dog, she just loves to make sure you're taken care of.

When we got to the school, it was already crowded. I guess people heard that if you came late you might not get a seat. It didn't take us long to set up and get into our costumes. Hey, we were pros now!

By the time of the show, we had sold a *bazillion* tickets. Everybody wanted to see the smartest dog on the planet! Including a lot of kids and parents who had already seen it the first time. Still no sign of Mr. Morris. I wondered what his errand could be that was so important that he'd miss our show? It wasn't like him to miss anything that involved his family.

The people from the TV studio came just like they said. Everyone wanted a seat, so that they might get in the picture. It was really cool to see the cameras up close. I always wanted to know how those things worked. The TV people said that our show would be on the evening news.

How cool is that? Now if we could just find someone with a TV 'cause the Morrises didn't have one. Maria, of course! Her family had TWO televisions. Oh, thank goodness!

Ant was in the yard selling "autographed" pictures of Sidney that he drew and Sidney signed with a muddy paw print. How cute was that! They sold like hot cakes. This time we all wanted to see what the other teams did, so we went to visit as many of them as we could. Some of them gave us free stuff. Must admit, the ice cream at "The Cream Team" stand, was the best I had ever eaten in my whole life.

We were definitely a lot more confident at this performance, even though there were twice as many people watching. Sam Lee, George and Joseph had even taught Sidney some new tricks, and Maria had glued rhinestones all over his robe and boxer shorts. Plus don't forget about the TV cameras! Just like before, Mrs. Morris was in the front row with Aunt Hattie and our cousins. But still no Mr. Morris. Weird. Oh well, the show must go on! Lights, cameras, Action!

Now if you thought the first show was good, today's show was even better! It was mostly the same except now we trusted Rodney enough to put him in charge of sound effects, music, and the whistle. Ant was okay with that. Boy. That kid was so happy, that he never stopped smiling. Please, he even took orders from ME!

Miss Dollywog couldn't take her eyes off of him, I guess she couldn't believe it, either.

Rodney even put his transistor radio up to the microphone so everyone could listen to music while we were setting up and during intermission. And that was HIS idea! Then it was time for our grand finale. You know the routine: Superhero, magic tricks, then the big fight with Sam Lee. Sidney jumped higher, twirled like a ballerina, and even barked like he was talking to the audience. The fight scene was even more incredible because this time, Sidney stood over Sam Lee when he "knocked him out" and licked his face. It was hilarious.

When Hector grabbed Sidney's front paw and announced him the champion of the world, the entire audience stood on their feet and cheered for what must have been five whole minutes. Sidney really surprised us, because he actually took a bow, (he just lowered his head) and waved his paw like the champ he was. Problem. Sidney got so excited that he peed on the floor. Oh well, it could have been worse. It could have been George! Sidney was a STAR! We were all STARS!

When the yard started to clear, me and my brothers ran over to our family. But to our surprise, there was Mr. Morris. He hadn't missed the show after all!

"Sorry, kids," he said. "But by the time we got back, all the seats up front were taken. So we had to watch from the back."

"Oh, that's okay, wait a minute. We? What do you mean WE?!" I asked.

Then Mr. Morris stepped aside and there was our Daddy, and our three brothers!

OH MY GOODNESS!!!

That's where he went, to get our dad and our brothers.

"Hey, *sweet pea!*" he said looking at me. "I'm so proud of you all! And your mama would be proud, too!"

We introduced our cousins to our Dad, and our brothers. Of course, everyone hugged — my gosh, hugging is like a cold — it's contagious. Miss Dollywog came over, and we even introduced her. She told us that all the teams sold mounds of stuff and made *goo-gobs* of money!

We did get asked to pose for pictures for the newspaper. Imagine that! I wanted to get everyone in the photo: The team; Mr. and Mrs. Morris; my brothers; my dad, Sidney ... everyone!

"Mom, Dad," I yelled, the words just rolled off my tongue. "There's a reporter who's waiting to interview us and take our picture. And Daddy, you have to be in the picture!"

YUP! From that day on, that's what we called the Morrises. MOM and DAD! I guess they earned it. And our Daddy was always "Daddy."

Daddy pulled me aside and said, "Sweet Pea, the Morrises are wonderful people, and it's great to hear you kids call them Mom and Dad, 'cause they love you all just like parents. *Ain't* no harm in loving folks back."

Mrs. Morris invited everyone back to our house. Mr. Morris had to make two trips to fit everybody in the car. We are a pretty big family, you know what I mean?

We talked about the show the entire ride home. We talked about it over cookies. We talked about it at dinner. We even talked about it after dinner. Our daddy and brothers spent the night. All us kids slept on the living room floor and the grown-ups slept in our beds.

Unfortunately all our cousins went home — no room for all *them folks.*

Shucks!

16

A Home of Our Own
by Emma

After the news got out that we were on TV, all the girls wanted to go to the graduation picnic with *Rodney-the-used-to-be-bully-who-turned-over-a-new-leaf-and-is-now-very-popular.* But he asked ME!

And, I said "yes."

If you had ever told me that one day I would go anywhere with **Rodney**, I would have thought you were crazy. Shoot, I would have thought that *I* was crazy. But like I said, now he was a totally different person. Plus he smiled a lot so all the girls got to see how cute he really was.

He still calls me Vanilla, though. But now he says it's "'cause I'm sweet like ice cream."

Sam Lee and CJ sort of started hanging around together. George and Joseph could care less about girls. They're still worried about getting cooties. Go figure.

Miss Gale (remember the robot lady from the foster agency?) eventually came to tell us good bye and that she wouldn't ever be taking us to a new home again. That was the best thing she ever said to us. She couldn't believe how different we looked. We weren't "skinny as rails" anymore. Especially Joseph who STILL sneaks bread off the table to eat before bedtime.

I think the reason why he doesn't suck his fingers anymore is because he's too busy trying to shove food in his mouth. And me? I stopped sucking my thumb. Not sure why, just one day I decided to stop, and I did. The Morrises said that when I get braces, my teeth will get straight.

As far as George goes, it was like he stopped peeing the bed the day we got Sidney. Boy, we are some happy kids.

To top it off, a few months later, Sidney and Loretta (that's the name of his Poodle friend) had puppies. Oops, I forgot to tell you, Loretta lived over by the railroad tracks, and it seems that Sidney had been sneaking out at night to visit her. At least that's what her owners told the Morrises.

So THAT'S where he kept disappearing to!

George called the puppies, *"Boxapoos,"* on account of Sidney being a Boxer and Loretta being a Poodle. As soon as they grow a little, the team said they will begin training them to do tricks like their famous dad. That way, they will be ready when Joseph is in the sixth grade.

Oh, and by the way, we made sure that we got a *trillion* copies of the newspaper article and pictures of the team with our family.

I cut it out and put it in the suitcase that holds all of our other special stuff. Doesn't look like we'll be using it ever again.

At last! We had a home of our own. My brothers George and Joseph, Daddy, our mom and dad, our dog Sidney, and a ton of cousins. Just like the families on TV. George was right, his powers were back!

WHO WOULD HAVE THUNK IT!!

Special acknowledgements to Dr. Donna Marie Jones for her dedication, diligence, wise counsel and patience in rereading the manuscript until we got it right.

about George C. Fraser

George C. Fraser is a popular speaker, entrepreneur and best-selling author of three books: *Success Runs in Our Race*; *Race For Success*; and *Click: Ten Truths for Building Extraordinary Relationships*. He is CEO of FraserNet, Inc., a company he founded over 25 years ago with the vision to lead a global networking movement that brings together diverse human resources to increase opportunities for people of African descent.

He graduated from the prestigious Dartmouth College Minority Business Executive Program. In 1999, he was awarded an Honorary Doctorate Degree of Humane Letters from Jarvis Christian College.

George is the Chairman of Phoenix Village Academy, which consists of three afro-centric charter schools that serve Cleveland's inner-city children. His views have been solicited by media as diverse as CNN and the Wall Street Journal.

He rose to leadership positions with Procter & Gamble, The United Way, and Ford Motor Company. UPSCALE magazine named him one of the "Top 50 Power Brokers in Black America."

George has appeared on seven national magazine covers and was recently inducted into The Minority Business Hall of Fame and Museum.

about Emma Fraser-Pendleton

Emma Fraser-Pendleton is a life coach, motivational speaker, author, ordained Minister, and former Assistant Superintendent of Schools. Currently she is a Project Director for Turnaround for Children, working in the most challenging schools in New York City.

Emma is the recipient of several prestigious scholarships. In 1989, she was awarded an academic Fellowship to the Harvard Graduate School of Education and a Ford Foundation fellowship to continue her studies at Harvard. At Harvard she served as a teaching fellow, and member of the faculty, and was a noted panelist on the International Forum of Changing Trends in Education.

Highlights of her career include: Designing and implementing a self-esteem program for women living in shelters; the Woman of Wisdom Award, Delta Sorority, 2010; Distinguished Black Women Award, BISA, 2009; the Barnes Historical Society and Queens Legend Award in 2004. In addition, Emma has also received the E.C. Reems Women's International Ministries Award and in 2005, The Hugh O'Brien Youth Leadership Award.

about Jerry Craft

Jerry Craft is a children's book writer, illustrator and the creator of Mama's Boyz, an award-winning comic strip that has been distributed by King Features Syndicate since 1995. He is one of the few syndicated African-American cartoonists in the country.

He has won three African American Literary Awards for best comic strip (2011, 2009 & 2004). Jerry has published three books based on his comic strip, illustrated 10 children's books and has had his work appear in Essence Magazine, Ebony, comic books, greeting cards, book covers, board games, transit ads and two *Chicken Soup for the African American Soul* books. He has also written and illustrated two novels: *The Offenders: Saving the World After Serving Detention* (middle grade) and *Positive Force* (Young Adult).

Jerry is the former editorial director of the Sports Illustrated for Kids website. When he is not at his drawing table, he teaches kids his cartooning and illustration techniques at schools and libraries across the country.

To learn more about Jerry's work, please visit his website at www.mamasboyz.com or email him at: jerrycraft@aol.com.